T0194050

THE WAIST GUNNER

A TALE OF WAR AND TRUE LOVE

ALAN VAN RANSOM

THE WAIST GUNNER
A TALE OF WAR AND TRUE LOVE

This is a work of fiction. All of the characters, names, incidents, organizations, and dialogue in this novel are either the products of the author's imagination or are used fictitiously.

iUniverse books may be ordered through booksellers or by contacting:

iUniverse
1663 Liberty Drive
Bloomington, IN 47403
www.iuniverse.com
1-800-Authors (1-800-288-4677)

ISBN: 978-1-5320-7000-6 (sc)
ISBN: 978-1-5320-6999-4 (e)

Library of Congress Control Number: 2019904020

Print information available on the last page.

iUniverse rev. date: 04/24/2019

For the troops. My gratitude for the men and women who died defending my family can never be expressed in words. I owe the deepest of every ounce of everything that my soul is worth to thank you for your service. This book is dedicated to your memory.

PROLOGUE

On September 3, 1939, Great Britain and France declared war on Germany. On June 24, 1940, France officially surrendered to Germany. The push by the Nazis and the Gestapo to enslave French people had caused an upheaval of French citizens to leave France, and many of that number escaped to as far away as Africa.

People in western France weren't as lucky as the people in the east inasmuch as the Nazis had formed blockades through the center of France. Most of the escapees from the west were enslaved, so this was a major deterrent for the majority of the citizens to want to take chances. They stayed put.

The good citizens of Saint-Nazaire, France, understood the need for survival, so they had begun to stockpile simple things like food, clothing, and even a few medical supplies. They used the old church at Ablain as a storage area. This was a very good idea since Saint-Nazaire was eventually put on one of the most major kill lists. The few survivors of the subsequent attack on the city were able to move into the crypt of the old church ruins and live off the supplies.

On May 18, 1941, Saint-Nazaire, France, was targeted for destruction by the Nazis. This campaign lasted for ten days, and the city was reduced to rubble. It was the only city in France that was 100 percent destroyed. The Germans needed this port city because of the massive shipbuilding and repair docks it offered. The town was targeted, but the docks were not. It was a prime location for building U-boats since it offered short routes to the various countries surrounding the area. The Nazis needed to protect their operations that were invading these countries using submarines—or U-boats, as they were called. Destroying the city of Saint-Nazaire would get rid of the possibility of infiltration by Allied groups, thereby preventing a coup from the citizens or the citizens employing the help of outsiders. So the savagery began. Collateral damage was necessary, and the Nazis were not polite about it.

Emma Bellerose and her family were nearly killed in the escape from the initial bombs that fell on the city. Her father and mother are Alexandre and Josephine, and her sisters are Alise and Sophie. When the bombing started, Emma was seventeen years old. Her sister Alise was the next oldest at eight years old. Sophie was the youngest at six years old.

The Bellerose family found refuge in the old abandoned church at Ablain and gathered other families that were left homeless and destitute from the devastation. Two years passed, and they were still in the church. They lived in the crypt and had fashioned furniture out of the stone rubble. One large dining room table was set up in the basement. They had to make do and were doing a pretty good job of it.

Bill McLaughton is a US military waist gunner. He has a persistent problem with a nightmare. Will he ever figure out what the nightmare means? In the meantime, he is assigned to an RAF bomber base in Polebrook, England. He is nineteen years old, and he was born and raised in the United States in Greenfield, Indiana. He has had a rather uninteresting life, but that is about to change.

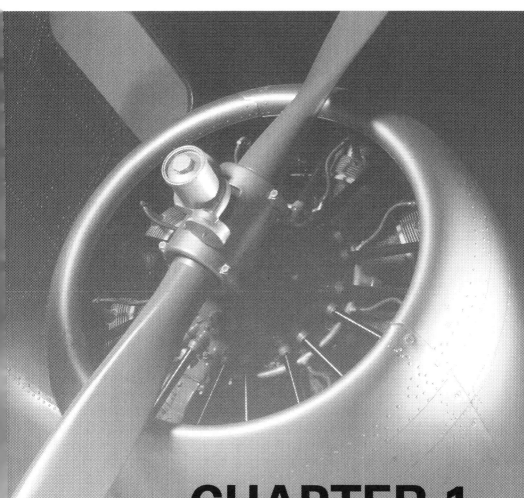

CHAPTER 1

E mma sat on what she would later refer to as her "perch." The perch was a stone platform that had served to hold the steeple of the old church, stone wreckage that had become home for the Bellerose family. It was the old ruined church on the hill. The church at Ablain had been a landmark since earlier in the decade. The family had taken refuge in the crypt of the church, which was still pretty much intact and gave them shelter from the elements. They had taken in other families to share in the shelter and now had a total of five families consisting of twenty-six men, women, and children living among them. The children had plenty of room to play in the remains of the old courtyard. The perch gave Emma a place of refuge to think and to ponder. It was her place of solitude. More importantly, it gave her a place to mourn.

Tonight was particularly difficult for Emma because it marked one month since the destruction of her beloved hometown. The reality of death haunted her with the sounds of tormented screams and the smell of burning flesh. The city of Saint-Nazaire now consisted of individual piles of rubble where homes and businesses once stood—a grim reminder that life was so very fragile. All her childhood memories seemed out of focus because of her inability to visit what was once a happy place—a place now reduced to nothingness. Her mind often returned to the days when she was content living with her family in a nice neighborhood and having happy conversations with friends who lived on the same street. Now, most of her friends were dead or in hiding, just like she and her family were.

She remembered the night the bombs fell. She and her sisters were awakened by shrieks and screams and the sounds of explosions as bombs found their mark.

Emma's father had burst through the bedroom door spouting unintelligible words.

Emma's mother ran into the room behind their father, sobbing uncontrollably, desperately trying to get to her daughters to carry them away from the impending danger. Her father had gotten to Alise first, and her mother grabbed Sophie off the bed they shared. As her parents held her two sisters, her father looked at her and said, "Get up. We must leave now!"

She remembered bursting out the front door of the house and making it to the street. People were running in confusion and trying to get away from the explosions. There were dead bodies in the street and the nearby yards. Some of the homes had already been destroyed. Her parents struggled to cover the eyes of her two sisters so they wouldn't see the horror that surrounded them. No one was there to cover her eyes. She was determined to help get her family to safety—no matter what it took. There would be time later, after they were safe, to grieve over the sight.

Another bomb struck the ground one hundred yards behind them. There was an acrid smell in the air, a combination of tar and burning flesh, and it choked her to smell it, but she had to press on. They had made it to the edge of the city and had started up the hill into the woods when there was a blinding flash.

Another bomb had exploded fifty yards to the side of them. The shock wave caused Emma to fall to the ground, and she immediately scrambled back to her feet as hot shrapnel whizzed past her. The bombing in the city had intensified, and the anguished screams and wails diminished as those who hadn't made it out perished. The family found a huddle of trees and collapsed in a heap to rest.

Emma remembered looking out over the water, which was clearly visible from atop the hill. There were many, many ships in a tremendous formation. Two of the larger ships were lighting the water as flashes appeared at various points from the guns that were all along the bows.

The brilliant flashes of light reminded her of having her picture taken with a camera. Other smaller boats had already begun to swarm the shore of the docks.

"Down, Emma!" Her father put his hand on her head and pulled her closer to the safety of his chest.

Emma was unable to speak as she choked back tears. Sophie and Alise were silent while being comforted by their mother. The bombing had slowed, but there were echoes of smaller explosions off in the distance.

The bombs finally stopped falling. There were no sounds from the city. There were no homes or businesses left standing at all. The only light was from the fire of burning buildings and small explosions from what she could only imagine were propane and gas tanks. The town was dead, and so were most of its inhabitants.

She looked back at the docks, which were now a bustle of activity. Men in uniforms were rushing up and down. After the initial group of soldiers had cleared the east end of the docks, one man remained. He was different. He wasn't wearing a pointy helmet like the rest of the men. This man was wearing a brim hat, and he looked official.

Emma watched as the man stood still and then reached down on his chest to grab his binoculars. He put them to his eyes and moved them back and forth. Emma had no idea what he was looking for. The man tilted his head back and stopped his gaze directly on Emma's family. He held his gaze there for several seconds before he put the binoculars back down on his chest.

A cold chill ran through Emma as she realized that evil had come to town. Emma remembered that night as she grimaced at the thought of the destruction. She thought of friends she would never see again. She thought of the little old lady next door who would smile and wave whenever they made eye contact. She grieved deeply for the losses. Emma put her face in her hands and wept, but the tears brought no consolation.

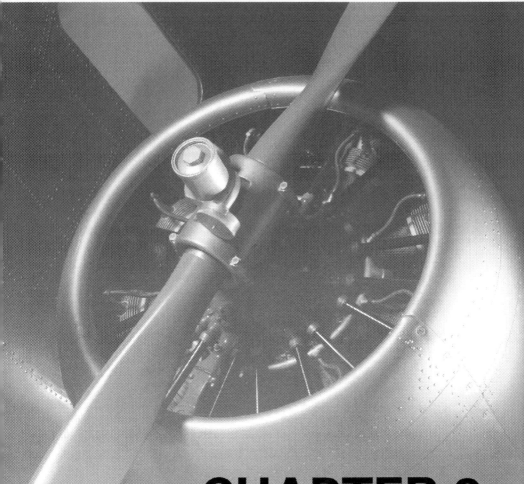

CHAPTER 2

The nightmare was always the same. Bill woke and bolted upright on his bunk. A bead of sweat dripped off his chin and down onto his T-shirt. His eyes were open, but there was no comprehension of what he was seeing. As his vision became clearer, he slowly realized that it was not the nightmare that had woken him at all. His ears were filled with the sounds of an alarm horn. Bill glanced at his watch. "Ah! 0237," he muttered, wondering whether he'd ever be able to get any sleep.

Apparently, the SS *John W. Brown* transport ship that he was on was under attack.

Bill swiveled sideways in the bunk and slipped on his boots.

From the bunk above, a voice said, "Don't let the alarm worry you."

Bill stood up and looked at the fellow in the bunk. He was about Bill's age, nineteen, and he was dressed in fatigues, suggesting that he was US military.

The young man smiled. "I'm Henry Jenkins." He extended his hand, which Bill took firmly.

"I'm Bill McLaughton."

The alarm went silent.

"Now we don't have to shout." Henry chuckled. "That stupid alarm has been on the fritz since the last time I sailed this ship."

Bill cocked his head to one side. "So, you've been on this ship before?"

Henry shifted off his back and swiveled around so that his feet were dangling off the bunk.

"Yep," he said, scratching his head. "I was shifted stateside from Australia. I've been called back to action. Headed to Polebrook, actually."

Bill looked at Henry. A look of true surprise spread across his face. Bill was also headed to Polebrook.

"Three Hundred Fifty-First Bombing Group?" Bill asked.

Henry turned his head slightly to the left and slanted his eyes inquisitively. "Yes. How did you know?"

It was Bill's turn to chuckle.

"Same here. Three Hundred Fifty-First Bomber Group and Five Hundred-Ninth Squadron."

Henry continued with the look of surprise as he stumbled for words.

"Five Hundred Seventh here. Small world, huh? Are you a pilot?"

Bill looked at the floor and shook his head. "Nah. I'm a waist gunner," he said as if he believed that Henry would think it was a job beneath what he expected. Waist gunners had the hard part. They stood next to an open window at midship with the freezing air rushing in. Most waist gunners suffered frostbite in the early days. The thick clothing and heated suits were helpful, but they didn't always work out as planned.

"I'm a rear turret gunner," Henry said. "I guess I have the easy part."

The conversation continued through the next hour or so as they discussed the danger and excitement of the missions that they would run. They wondered where they would be sent and what the outcome would be. The dimly lit bunk room became a haven for thoughts, fears, and even the hopes of the two men who were destined to become the best of friends.

Emma sat at the dinner table in silence and stared at her plate. Somehow, the venison and various fruits and vegetables didn't seem to woo her hunger. It had been two years since the bombing of her beloved town, and she was still in mourning. Survivors guilt, maybe? She battled against the thoughts that had haunted her for the past two years. The people who'd brought this suffering on these poor folks were going to pay for what they did. She then had to bite back against her anger as this thought made her feel as if she were no better than they were. She considered herself a true lady, and if that meant she had to accept things the way they had turned out, then so be it!

Emma looked around the table at the various families as they intermingled with one another. She often marveled at these dinners how such a tragedy had brought all these people together as one big family. The adults engaged in a banter that would sometimes erupt in laughter. The younger people talked in small groups about things that only teenagers discussed. The children did the usual random frivolous playful things together. Healing had seemed to take root, but there was still a big hole in Emma's heart that would probably never heal. She no longer had any hope of it healing at least.

"Eat your dinner before it gets cold," said a voice from behind her.

Emma turned around to see her mother.

"I'm not hungry, Mother," she replied.

Her mother moved on down the table to check on the others, offering a comment over her shoulder. "You need to eat, child!"

Food was the last thing on Emma's mind. What she really wanted to do was to climb up on her perch and let her mind wander away from all the wreckage and the Nazi-occupied docks and even as far off as the center of the ocean. She imagined that the sea would offer more peace than she'd ever seen. The perch was her little private sanctuary. She could have privacy and tune out all the hustle and bustle of the children playing, the women cooking and cleaning, and the men laughing and joking. She wanted solitude. Actually, she wanted someone to share her solitude. Shared solitude. Was that even possible?

Emma stood up from the table and wandered up the stairs to the ruins. It was twilight. It was the time she longed to be alone. She climbed up to the perch and started the process of blocking out all the confusion of the people downstairs. This was a peaceful time for her, and yet it also brought back memories of death and destruction. Choking back tears, she remembered the good times. And they were good times too! Going to school with friends and having lunch together in the school cafeteria; walking home after school and carrying on conversations that caused her and her friends to giggle like the innocent young teenagers they were; talking about boys—who was dating whom, who was breaking up with whom. And now that was all gone. None of those close friends had survived the attack two short years ago.

This was her perch, her place of solitude. No one ever bothered her here, so she could grieve and cry and rejoice in total privacy. However, there was not that much to rejoice about. It was a place of soul cleansing and emotional release, a place for the beginning of the long process of healing.

CHAPTER 3

May 5, 1943, 0500

Bill opened his eyes. He was on his bunk in the barracks at the Polebrook Bomber Base. The base was designed to hold two hundred airmen, and there were twenty barracks holding each individual flight crew. Each bomber group was housed with their own teammates. The barracks were designed for ten men each since there were ten crew members per bomber.

Bill rubbed his eyes, turned sideways, and put his bare feet on the floor.

By this time the other men had begun to rouse. Some of them grumbled and complained about the way the bunk had treated them during the night.

One man in a bunk next to the doorway stood up and shook his head. "Stop grousing, you bunch of spoiled ingrates! The bunks ain't that bad!" The unidentified man—at least at this point—then turned his attention to

Bill. With his head cocked to one side, he seemed to size up the newbie. "So, what do we have here?" he posed. There was a pause as he looked up and down Bill's frame as if he were prey.

Bill had the impression that he was about to be chewed up and spit out. This thought gave him the creeps. He found himself wishing for a hole to open in the surface beneath him, floor included, so that his body could be sucked into the ground, never to be heard from again. Anything was better than being sized up for a meal.

"I'm Lieutenant C. J. Russell. And what would be your name?"

Bill felt as if the question had been put up in the air for anyone to answer. He looked around the room, possibly to see if anyone was going to throw him a lifeline. No lifeline? Bill quickly realized by the blank expressions, some smirks, and even some shaking of heads that he was all alone. The lieutenant took a step toward Bill, with his hands on his hips and a glare that would scare the dead.

Bill immediately stood up, very quickly, and bumped his shoulder into the top bunk. The pain was excruciating, but he was determined at this point of the game to not let it show. Besides, he didn't want any weakness to be on display. Nope. *Let's keep that long list of weaknesses hidden!*

"I asked you a question, son! What … is … your … name?" The lieutenant still had his hands on his hips, and his knuckles whitened as he clenched his waist. It would have appeared to even the novice that the slow burn was about to become a full-on mushroom cloud.

Bill sucked in his gut and protruded his chest outward as far as he could so that he looked tougher than he actually was.

"Sergeant William C. McLaughton, Lieutenant! I'm trained as a waist gunner!" Bill blurted with all the force he could muster. He honestly thought he was going to wet his pants in the process of forming his first words to the angry man.

The lieutenant continued glaring at Bill.

Just punch me and get it over with, thought Bill. This was the most uncomfortable he had ever felt. He was humiliated—not only because of the exchange but because he had overplayed his reply to the angry lieutenant.

The lieutenant then relaxed his face, and a big smile appeared. "At ease, son! I'm just screwing with you! I couldn't resist breaking you in. You look mighty tasty, but it's too close to breakfast for me to ruin my appetite." The lieutenant patted Bill on the shoulder.

A short round of laughter filled the room and then quickly subsided.

Bill was relieved that he had been spared the death of being stared down. He let out a long sigh.

The lieutenant folded his arms across his chest and said, "I guess introductions are needed here."

All the men in the room stood.

"To your left is the copilot. His name is James Hawthorne, more commonly referred to as 'Jim' or 'Jimmy Boy.'"

"Thanks for the intro, Lieutenant, but you'll never get 'Jimmy Boy' to stick," Jim said with a smirk back at the lieutenant.

A round of laughter erupted, but once again, it subsided as quickly as it had begun.

"Next is going to be your partner in crime, the guy who will be next to you on the flight. Sam Brighton. He's also a waist gunner," said the lieutenant.

The introductions continued until all had been presented to Bill. The next few minutes were spent with the team chatting among themselves and welcoming the newbie.

Bill felt at home. He had been accepted, and that's all that mattered. A team of ten men on a plane fighting for the same goal had to be a club. And Bill was certainly welcomed to the club.

The lieutenant said, "Okay. Enough of this. Let's get to breakfast. Now!"

The group became silent and started moving toward the front door of the barracks. Bill fell into the line and tried to seem like one of the gang. The very last thing he wanted to do was be different.

After they cleared the door, the group disbanded and then huddled back together as they made their way to the mess hall. They talked about this and that, and they even included Bill in the conversation. Even though he wasn't in Indiana, he still felt the closeness of home.

As they reached the mess hall, Bill looked through the window and saw his friend Henry at one of the tables. Henry looked up and saw Bill, and they exchanged nods. As they entered, the smell of bacon and coffee permeated the air. Bill got a tray of food and went over to join Henry.

"Top of the mornin'," Bill said with a grin.

"Howdy, Bill." Henry took a sip of his coffee.

"I guess we're both scheduled to fly today." Bill sat down and tried to get comfortable on the steel seat. He made a grumbly remark about the hard stool.

"Yeah, I s'pose," Henry said. "Wonder what the temperature is s'posed to be?"

Bill wrinkled his face and shook his head. "Forties?"

"That's a little cold for my pleasure," Henry said. "I'd hate to be standing next to that open window at twenty-three thousand feet."

"Yeah. It won't be comfortable—but probably more comfortable than this seat," Bill said as he bobbed up and down.

Both men laughed, but the mirth turned to serious concentration on the tasks at hand as they realized the dangers ahead of them. The wide-open, clear blue sky had black polka dots of antiaircraft shells peppering the serene blueness. The fighter planes looked like an entertaining spectacle until one realized that those planes were weapons of death.

The men realized that this was now the real deal. All the training they had received in their schools had been exciting, but now the excitement was gone. Realization had set in and it was, for lack of a better word, terrifying.

Bill ate his breakfast and Henry sipped his coffee, both in silence, as they sat lost in their own thoughts of the day's bombing raids.

Bill finished all but two slices of bacon and half of a piece of toast. He folded the bacon as tightly as he could and tried to wrap the toast around the roll.

Henry had finished his coffee and was blankly staring into the empty cup as he slowly spun it in circles, watching the last few drops do a dance around the bottom. "This is going to be an interesting day," Henry said, never taking his eyes off the dancing drops.

May 5, 1943, 0930

Josephine Bellerose sat at the massive stone dinner table with her husband, Alexandre. Josephine had always had concerns for the welfare of her family, and it was not unusual for her to be in deep thought, seemingly off in a distant place.

Alexandre sat for several minutes, rubbing his finger on the lip of his cup, which was now empty. He stared at his wife, contemplating the proper time to interrupt her thoughts with the usual questions.

"What are you thinking about, dear?"

Josephine snapped out of her trance.

"I'm sorry, what did you say?"

"I asked you what you were thinking about. I don't mean to pry, but you seem worried."

Josephine looked at her cup and frowned. She didn't mind talking to Alexandre about her thoughts, but what she had been thinking just then would cause her pain just to say it. It was painful enough to think about it;

saying it would be exponentially worse. Josephine drew in a deep breath and looked at Alexandre.

"It's Emma."

"Yes. I've been concerned about her as well. She's become a bit reclusive."

"She's constantly in a sad state. She seems depressed," Josephine said, putting her hand on the table as she spoke.

Alexandre pondered for a moment. He was a levelheaded man and had a good relationship with his daughters. They loved both him and Josephine, and they had known since the night of the bombing that they would lay down their lives for their girls no matter what it took.

Alexandre said, "I'm going to take Emma under my wing."

Josephine had no idea what he was talking about.

"What do you mean?"

"Emma needs to go hunting with me for the afternoon."

"Hunting? And that's your solution?"

"Yes. It will be good for her to get out and about. She's been cooped up here for too long. Sophie and Alise have adjusted and made friends here. Emma doesn't have anyone her age to talk to."

Josephine looked back down at her cup and was silent for a moment. Her face furrowed as if she were thinking very deeply. Alexandre was right, but why would taking her hunting be a good thing? Perhaps being cooped up there too long had made the hole in her heart even bigger. Being away from there would be good. At least Josephine hoped so. "Take Emma hunting," Josephine said after her long contemplation. "I've always trusted your judgment. Since the day we were married, I've never mistrusted you—and you've never let me down."

Alexandre gave a half smile and nodded. He was sure it was the right road to take to snap Emma out of her depression. Since the night the bombs fell, Emma had been stuck in this place without venturing out. Her perch was a grim reminder of the events that had occurred on that terrible night. Her perch may have been her place of solitude and contemplation, but it was also a place of self-torment.

May 5, 1943, 1145

Bill stepped onto the B-17 bomber that would be his work space for the afternoon. He had dressed in the warm suit that had been provided for him—along with the flak jacket that seemed to be a little too itchy for his liking.

"Is this your first mission?" Sam asked.

"Yeah," Bill said. "I'm a bit of a nervous wreck."

"You'll do fine!" Sam smiled so that Bill would feel more comfortable.

"I've flown in practice—but never on a mission." Bill was trying not to sound like he was too much of a newbie.

Lieutenant Russell stepped aboard the plane and said, "Listen up! Wheels up in one hour! Get your preflight done—and make sure all your equipment is working as it's supposed to. Give me your reports no later than fifteen minutes before takeoff!"

Bill reached his station and checked his gun to make sure it was free of grit and grime. It was. Was it full of ammo? It was. There was just something about a .30-caliber round that he liked. It had a nice recoil and wasn't overpowering like the .50-caliber. The nice, large round would rip through the skin of an enemy aircraft like it was tearing into scrap paper. He just had to make sure his aim was sure. *Lead the target! Never follow!* His mind was going in a million directions, but he had to concentrate. There was no room for error, and he wasn't about to make room.

May 5, 1943, 1200

Emma's father looked at her and smiled.

Emma looked back and gave a smile that she had to force, trying to make it look as sincere as possible.

"Your mother is concerned for your well-being. I don't mean to torture you by bringing you out here," her father said in a comforting voice.

"I enjoy our time together, Father. But did it have to be hunting?"

"Well, we could have gone fishing, but the Nazis don't really like us to be on the shoreline."

"I understand," she said with contempt in her voice. "And I would prefer not to have them around either." The contempt was for the Nazis. She had tried to control her hatred for the past two years, but the feeling had welled up too many times and was now part of her.

Alexandre completely understood what she meant. After the murder and debauchery that had transpired, Alexandre had total empathy for why she thought the way she did.

"Let's go to the trench to check on our traps."

The trench was a short distance across the top of the hill. It was almost totally invisible to the Nazis, and the Nazis didn't much care what the locals did as far as farming and trapping was concerned—as long as no one came close to the docks. This disinterest was a saving grace for the locals. Without food, they would have been dead a long time ago. After the Nazi invasion, France was blockaded, and not much trade was done between the cities. Thus, many of the people died due to starvation and disease.

They had made it to the trench, but none of the traps were sprung. Emma breathed a sigh of relief. She didn't want to have to kill an animal, much less field dress one.

The traps were a bit of overkill. They were actually bear traps that had been left over from hunting expeditions from the men of the town before it was destroyed. Catching a deer in a bear trap was like killing a mosquito with a hammer. It mangled the legs and caused a great deal of suffering. But what else could they do?

"Looks like we've got tracks here but no catch," her father said. "We may as well go pick some berries."

May 5, 1943, 1300

Bill felt the movement of the plane as it taxied to the runway. Other planes were ahead of theirs, twelve to be exact, but it wouldn't take long once they got the flow of takeoffs started. There were twenty planes scheduled to drop bombs on the docks at Saint-Nazaire, France. The bombing run would take five hours.

Over the headsets, he could hear the pilot and the copilot prepping for takeoff.

"Check generators for ampere output!"

"Ampere output okay!"

"Check voltage on the generators!"

"Twenty-eight and a half on all four!"

Tests continued to the end of the checklist, and then the pilot called to the tower for clearance to take off.

It was their turn to roll.

Bill could feel the butterflies fluttering around in his gut as they rolled down the runway. He could see the markers going by faster and faster. Finally, at 120 miles per hour, they took off and began their climb. They leveled off at twenty-three thousand feet and 160 miles per hour. Two and a half hours to the target.

May 5, 1943, 1500

The sky was myriad shades of blue, and Emma was caught up in the radiant colors. They seemed to be deep blue directly overhead but softened to milder shades as they approached the horizon. The changes in the shades reminded her of a ribbon. The light and wispy clouds were like a halo, surrounding the horizon and then tapering off to a bald and very blue spot directly above her. Emma smiled as she witnessed this beautiful sight; she realized that there was indeed beauty in this world. Nature had a way of healing itself from the scars of warring humans.

Alexandre glanced over at Emma. The smile on her face was a refreshing sight.

"You know, these berries won't just pick themselves."

Emma looked down at her basket. It was empty. "I'm sorry, Father. I was caught up in my own thoughts."

"It's okay. Take your time and enjoy the sights."

Alexandre had been correct about bringing Emma out into nature. He knew that it would pick up her spirits, and after such a long time of her being withdrawn, it was exactly what she needed. Alexandre couldn't wait for Josephine to see the smile on Emma's face.

May 5, 1943, 1530

Bill heard the pilot, Lieutenant C. J. Russell, come over the headsets.

"Keep those guns sharp! We're ten minutes from the drop point!"

The sky had begun to fill with distant sights of enemy fighters. Bill looked out over the sea of bombers and prayed for the safety of them all, including his. Bill was the left waist gunner. He glanced at Sam, who was the right.

Sam said, "Look sharp, kid. This is where the fun starts."

The outer line of bombers was firing from the ball turrets and the left waist positions. The enemy fighters scattered to evade the fire and began to draw in behind the bomber group.

"Lead the target. Lead the target. Lead the target," Bill muttered to himself.

The rear gunner turret reported ten bandits one hundred yards above and to the tail.

Sam squeezed off a five-second round of fire up and to the right. "Two bandits hit and smoking!"

There was a sound like rain falling on a tin roof. The top of the ship had been hit with a hail of bullets. No one seemed to be alarmed over this fact, so Bill returned his attention to the gun. Two of the enemy aircraft had turned their attention to the left side of the ship, and they were already firing at the ship that was in front of and to the right of Bill's position. Bill squeezed off a few rounds while the words "lead the target" echoed in his mind.

The lead bandit was hit and had started to burn. The bandit that was above and behind the damaged bandit rolled to the left to avoid being hit by metal that had already begun to peel off Bill's target. Bill noticed that the plane he had hit was not changing position. He looked at the canopy and saw a large spray of blood covering the inside of the bubble.

Bill stepped back from the gun. "I *killed* someone."

Sam turned to look at Bill. Realizing that the safety of the ship required concentration, he put his hand on Bill's shoulder.

"First person you ever killed?"

Bill nodded.

"Think about it … a lot. You'll get used to it."

Sam turned back to his own gun and was immediately struck in the chest and the left shoulder with bullets. He fell to the floor, unable to make any sounds.

"Gunner down!" screamed Bill.

The radio officer immediately left his post and took over Sam's position.

Bill realized then and there that it was impossible to care for the injured when hands were short in the defense of the ship.

Bill glanced back down at Sam, who was gurgling and struggling to breathe. The gurgling stopped, and Sam went limp. The vacant look in his eyes was a haunting realization that friends were temporary.

The bandits were thinning slightly, but Bill had a renewed resolve. One of his newest friends, a member of his own crew, had been killed by an enemy that was hell-bent on killing them all. Bill was angry. He grabbed his gun and squeezed the trigger as tightly as he could. Two more bandits were on fire, and one more was smoking, but it wasn't enough to cover the anguish and hatred he felt in his gut.

The plane shook violently as a shell ripped off the bomb bay doors, the ball turret, and Sergeant Bader. A fire raged in the bomb bay. Two of the engines were immediately knocked out, and they had to fall out of formation. The plane was being attacked by several FW-190s, and they were able to fire at will.

Lieutenant Russell put the plane into a dive to extinguish the flames. Suddenly, the number three engine started running away, and the lieutenant had no choice but to give the order to abandon ship.

Bill had been knocked to the floor and was struggling to get back up. He had shrapnel in his left shoulder that rendered his left arm almost useless. Blood dripped from his face onto his freezer suit. He was unsure of how much injury he had sustained or what had struck him.

Bill worked to get the suit off his body so that his parachute would work. Struggling and screaming in pain, he worked his way to the cockpit.

There was an M1911 pistol sliding back and forth across the floor and Bill grabbed it and put it in the side pouch on his parachute pack. Finding the hatch to the nose section, he slithered into the hole of the nose gunner's compartment and fell through it. Unsure of his altitude, he pulled the cord. The chute opened, and the straps between his legs absorbed the impact of the sudden deceleration. Bill let out a bloodcurdling scream and then passed out from the agony.

May 5, 1943, 1540

The steady drone of the planes overhead had become obvious, and Emma once again looked skyward. She could see the polka dots of the planes off in the distance. The serene blue sky was now pockmarked with black circles that were appearing and disappearing sporadically. "Father?"

"Yes, child. I see." Alexandre pulled Emma close. "Stay right here and don't wander."

Emma put her arm around her father's waist. If there was impending danger, she didn't want to face it alone. She didn't want her father to be alone either. The droning of the many planes was closer now. There were black tubes below the larger ones. It looked like the planes were giving birth.

Alexandre was unsure of what was taking place. All he knew was that he wanted to protect his daughter.

Two of the men from the church home had come outside to see what was happening. One of them called for Alexandre.

"Yes. I'm here," Alexandre called back while turning to see the men.

The one who had called out was Father Ambroise. He had been a minister to the town of Saint-Nazaire.

The men ran to the side of Alexandre and Emma.

"What's going on here?" inquired Father Ambroise anxiously.

"A bombing raid," Alexandre said.

"As if we haven't seen enough of this?"

"It's the Americans—or the English. They're not here to hurt us. They're here to take out the Nazis," Alexandre said as if he were giving a prophesy.

The men of the church home were always amazed at Alexandre's intelligence. It was as if he were ahead of his time. They had learned to trust his instincts.

The first bombs began striking the docks. A steady cadence of *whump … whump … whump* could be heard. The group crouched down to watch the bombing. It was already too late to head back to the church. They'd have to wait it out there between the trees.

The concussive waves came in a steady rhythm. Suddenly, there was a thump behind them, seemingly off in the distance. They all turned to look, and there was a plume of smoke just up on the next rise.

"That was only two or three miles away," Father Ambroise said.

"We can worry about that later." Alexandre turned to look back at the docks. "Just stay down for now."

May 5, 1943, 1550

Bill had faded in and out of consciousness for the past few seconds. The wind had picked up and had drifted him in toward the shoreline of Saint-Nazaire. The devastating blows of the bombs falling had shifted his attention off what was falling out of the sky and on the destruction at hand. It was as if an angel had put her loving hands around him and had kept him safe.

The shoreline was imminent. He tried to clear his mind enough to estimate the seconds before impact. He counted five … four … and had miscalculated. His body, attached to the parachute, hit the water with more force than he had anticipated. The parachute then dragged him across the water like a skier. The jolting of his body against the waves was very painful, but at that point, he had resigned himself to death. It really didn't matter to him.

He finally reached the shore as the parachute, still catching the breeze, pulled him across the beach and into the brush and to a rest. Bill was unable to release himself from the parachute, and it just flapped and fluttered in the wind. He really didn't care if it dragged him halfway to China. He could hear the bombs pounding the docks, and he could feel the shock waves from the impacts rippling through his almost-lifeless body. As he laid there, he remembered his friend Henry and wondered if his mission had gone as planned. Many thoughts were in his mind. So much had happened in the past few days. He slowly drifted back into unconsciousness.

Emma tugged on her father's arm. "Look, Father, over there."

Father looked out across the water and saw Bill's parachute, with Bill attached, drifting down toward the waves. They watched as he was dragged ashore. He didn't move. They knew they needed to help him but were unsure if he was a friend or a foe.

"We need to help this man," Alexandre said with a look of compassion on his face.

"How are we going to do that? The Nazis will be onto us!"

"Head back to the church, Emma," Alexandre said. "Tell Mother to prepare for an injured man."

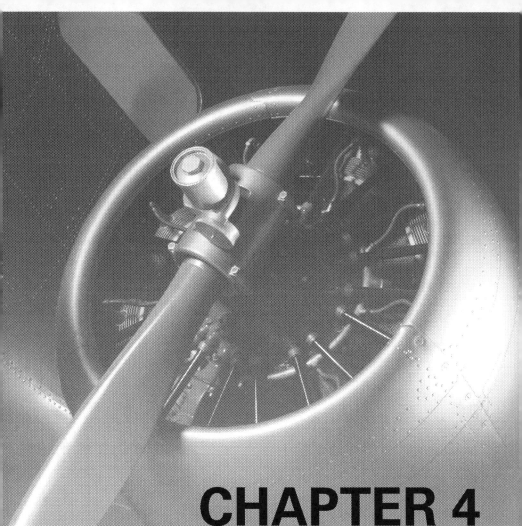

CHAPTER 4

The nightmare was always the same: the ball of fire, the eyes with flames for eyelids, and the fiery hands outstretched with the palms facing the heavens. Bill felt as if an electrical shock had just gone through his body as a quick convulsion jolted him awake. He usually awakened in an upright position when the nightmare occurred, but not this time.

"Ah. I see you're awake!" came an unknown voice from inside the haze.

Bill quickly realized that he had survived his ordeal. He was unsure of what situation he was in though. Was this a Nazi interrogation? Bill's eyesight focused, and he could see a man seated in a chair by a door. Bill was in a room and obviously on a bed. He was strapped down. After a quick observation, Bill realized that he was not in a prison cell. No bars on the windows. In fact, there were no windows at all. The door was not made of steel. There were no armed guards present. There were pictures on the wall, some of gardens, others of portraits.

A man who was across from him sensed his apprehension. He smiled at Bill to relieve his doubts.

"Don't be alarmed, my friend," said the man. "We'll get those straps off you."

"Why am I strapped to the bed?" Bill said.

"My name is Alexandre Bellerose, by the way. When we brought you in, you were convulsing. We had to strap you down to keep you from injuring yourself more. We had very little hope that you would survive, but you surprised us all. May I ask your name?"

"William C. McLaughton, sir!" he replied, trying to sound official. "People call me Bill."

He had no idea why he had replied in such an official tone. He guessed it was just one of his idiosyncrasies. He'd have to work on that.

"Very well, Bill. You can call me Alexandre."

"How long have I been out, sir?" Bill said, trying to sound the opposite of official. In his effort to sound unofficial, his voice cracked and made him sound weak.

"Seventeen days. You suffered some very grave injuries, a broken collarbone, and we had to remove a small amount of metal from your left shoulder."

Bill drew in a deep breath upon hearing the list. But Alexandre was not done.

"You also suffered a head injury. You had been struck by some sort of a solid object. Your left eye was swollen completely shut," continued Alexandre. "We're not doctors here, but we do have one of our friends who is a veterinarian, Rabiah Kaffenberger."

"A veterinarian?" Bill asked as his face wrinkled from the idea of a horse doctor working on his body.

"Yes," replied Alexandre. He stood up and opened the door. "Excuse me for a moment." Alexandre called out, "Josephine, will you please fetch this young man some food? He is finally awake."

There were apparently several people in the next room, and Bill heard a joyous eruption.

"And please send Rabiah in here," Alexandre said before closing the door. "You'll find that the ladies in this church home are wonderful cooks," Alexandre said with a big smile. He patted his stomach as if to indicate that it was one of the happier organs in his body.

There was a rap at the door, and Alexandre said, "Come. Come."

A man opened the door and came in. He smiled at Bill, clasped both of his hands in front of him, and spoke in a very cheerful voice.

"And how is our little patient today?"

Bill fought off the urge to whinny like a horse. Instead, he said, "Been better, been worse."

There was a short chuckle between the two men in the room with Bill. Even though what he had said wasn't that funny, they wanted to keep the mood light to make Bill more comfortable.

Rabiah lifted the blanket and examined Bill's shoulder. He wrinkled his face a little and said, "Ah. We're healing nicely. Another few weeks, and you'll be as good as new."

Bill looked at Rabiah. He had many questions for the good-natured horse doctor. He just didn't know how to phrase them.

There was a rap at the door.

Alexandre opened the door, and a woman stood there with a plate of food. Alexandre stepped aside and let her in.

Bill smiled at her.

She smiled back at him, set the plate on the bedside table, curtsied to Bill, and made her exit.

Bill looked over at the food and began to wonder how he was ever going to feed himself.

Alexandre, sensing the conundrum, leaned sideways in his chair and opened the door. "Emma, come here please."

As the door was already open, Rabiah made his exit.

"We'll talk later, young man."

Rabiah winked as he left the room.

"Yes, Father?"

Alexandre, obviously sensing that his daughter was uncomfortable, attempted to put her at ease.

"This young man is Bill. He is hungry and cannot feed himself. Will you do the honors?"

"Yes, Father." The young woman spoke softly and looked away. Her bashfulness was unmistakable. She turned a deeper shade of red than Bill could ever remember seeing anyone become. An interest sparked inside of him, and he looked her over.

Bill had never seen such a beautiful young lady. Her blonde hair and blue eyes were something that closely resembled one of the pretty ladies on the calendars in the barracks. Not the naughty ones, but the ones that showed pure beauty at its finest. He had dated a few pretty girls before he joined the air force, but none were as radiant as the one who stood before him now.

The girl stepped forward, averting her gaze to avoid embarrassment. She then looked at Bill. She cleared her throat as if to speak, but no words made their way out of her mouth.

Alexandre, looking suddenly uncomfortable, cleared his throat and said, "I'll leave you to your meal, sir. We'll talk later."

Bill nodded, and Alexandre made his exit.

Bill and Emma were alone in the room. They both felt very uncomfortable. It was anybody's guess that Alexandre had either forgotten, or temporarily lost his manners, to introduce the two young people. After a short time of silence, Bill said, "I'm Bill."

Bill already knew that the girl's name was Emma, but a formal introduction was never offered.

"I'm Emma," she replied nervously and averted her gaze once more. Emma pulled the chair next to the bed and picked up the plate of food. She scooped up the first forkful and put it in Bill's mouth, slowly and carefully.

Bill chewed the food. He was unable to take his gaze off Emma. Emma scooped up the second forkful, and as she approached Bill's mouth, Bill gently took her hand. "Is this as uncomfortable for you as it is for me?"

"I'm not uncomfortable," Emma replied.

This remark was obviously a lie, and Bill had seen right through it.

There was a pause.

"I don't want you to be uncomfortable. And I do have a confession to make," Bill said. "I am embarrassed to have to have someone feed me."

Emma smiled at the confession. She put the forkful in Bill's mouth and said, "I haven't been near a young man since the town was destroyed—so please forgive me if I seem standoffish."

CHAPTER 5

Lieutenant Adelbert Spangler was standing on the east dock when the transport boat pulled in. General Major Josef Kramer was on the boat, and Spangler was none too pleased that he was visiting his facility. Their history ran deep, and there was no love lost between them.

General Major Josef Kramer had been on the German battleship *Tirpitz* when Saint-Nazaire was destroyed. After the initial salvos were fired, he had ordered additional shells to be fired at the already-dead city. He had supervised the initial inspection of the damage. He had stood on the dock and surveyed the area, including the remaining population as they fled. He had seen the Bellerose family and had chuckled with glee that he had killed so many,

The general major stepped off the boat, took one look at Spangler, and snorted.

"Nice to see you too, General Major," Spangler said in an obvious attempt not to appear condescending. The tone was condescending, nonetheless.

"*Nice* wouldn't have been the word I used for you," said Kramer.

"It wasn't the first word that came to my mind either, sir, but there is a certain protocol to be used when addressing a superior officer."

"You're lazy and incompetent, Spangler. Show me the work that you haven't completed in repairing the facility—and then convince me that I shouldn't have you hanged!"

They walked a few steps, and Kramer gazed upon the ashes of Saint-Nazaire. The night of the blazing buildings and the screams of the terrified populace thrilled him to recall. He smiled like an idiot.

"Care to share your thoughts, General Major?" Spangler said.

"Just remembering the night I destroyed this wretched town," Kramer said with a hideous grin on his face.

They had stopped walking for a moment so Kramer could admire his handiwork. Spangler stared at the surface of the dock and said, "Beauty to ashes."

Kramer looked at Spangler with confusion on his face. "What did you say?"

"I said, 'Beauty to ashes.'"

"You should have said, 'Ashes to beauty.' These were not German people, so they are considered ashes. Burning their city down was pure beauty! Always remember that!"

Spangler cringed at the thought of what Kramer suggested. Even though he, himself, was a Nazi, he couldn't agree with what Kramer had described. They continued their walk, in silence, and entered the area where the construction was taking place.

Kramer once again smiled at the sight of the Jewish people slaving away while Nazi soldiers moved about with their rifles and at the sound of the groans of the overburdened workers as they struggled to work.

The Jews were malnourished and rail thin. One could see the rib cages on all of them. They all looked as though they were near death, and one would wonder how any work was being completed.

Soldiers rushed to the side of a Jewish woman who had collapsed on the ground.

"My wife! My wife!" exclaimed one of the Jewish men as he rushed to her side.

The soldiers beat them both to death with the butts of their rifles.

Kramer looked at Spangler. "It's a good thing we have an almost limitless supply of these wretched scum!"

Bill woke in a drenching sweat. His breathing was deep and fast. There was a rap on the door, and Bill gasped at the sound.

The door opened, and Alexandre stuck his head in with a concerned look on his face. "Are you okay?"

"I think so. Just a bad dream."

His breathing and heartbeat slowed down a little, and he was relieved to know that whatever had bothered his sleep had now gone away.

"May I come in?" inquired Alexandre as he slipped through the door and motioned toward the seat next to the opening.

"Of course. I could use the company."

Alexandre took a seat in the chair, which was now back against the wall next to the door. There was a pause as Alexandre wrinkled his face and cocked his head to one side. He was unsure as to how he was going to make an offer of help to Bill.

"We heard you shout, and we didn't know what to make of it. Bad dream?"

Bill nodded and let out a long sigh. "I have a recurring nightmare that I can't explain without sounding strange."

"Far be it for me to ever pry, but I will listen if you care to share the nightmare," Alexandre said, trying to be as diplomatic as possible.

Bill drew a deep breath and began recounting the events involved in the dream, or at least what he could recall. "It's unclear where I am. There are no sounds or movements around me. It's like a private theater, and no one is there to explain what is happening." Bill paused for a moment as if in pain from the memory. "There is a ball of fire. It's like a face, but it's not symmetrical. It looks like a tube is protruding down from the main ball. Branches stick out to the sides, and flames leap from the ends of the branches. The face has two eyes with flames for eyelids. The ball appears to be smiling. It's like a demon." Bill paused, shaking his head. "I don't know what to make of it."

After a short time, Alexandre said, "The demon seems like an inner struggle." Alexandre paused for a moment. "Can you tell me something about your childhood?"

Bill's father had died in an accident when he was working at a steel mill. A boiler exploded while his father was standing at his station directly in front of the boiler hatch. It had been explained to Bill, and he had developed his own vision of how the accident had taken place.

Bill began to describe the accident to Alexandre. "I was nine when my father was killed in an accident on the job. Management had been warned that the equipment needed replacement, and the vents on the boiler needed to be cleaned. They ignored the warnings. The boiler's pressure was too high, and the hatch blew off. My father was hit by the hatch and was crushed between it and a concrete wall. The fire in the boiler was white-hot."

It was as if Bill had had a breakthrough. It all became very clear to him then. The fire in the boiler was indeed his demon. He wasn't totally convinced about how it was all set up, but it was close enough. He was desperate at this point to get that nagging nightmare figured out.

Bill was so transfixed that he'd forgotten that Alexandre was in the room.

"You seem very deep in thought, Bill."

"Yes. Sorry, sir. I was busy convincing myself that my demon was created by my imagination."

"Imagination?" Alexandre said. "Imagination is for the conscious mind. Dreams are for the subconscious. How long have you been having this nightmare?"

"For about two years."

Alexandre leaned forward in his chair and put his fingertips together and his elbows on his knees. He squinted his eyes in deep thought. Alexandre's posture and expression unnerved Bill, and he tried to move away but was unable. Alexandre continued his deep thoughts for what seemed like an eternity, yet Bill remained silent.

Alexandre then began speaking. "Nightmares are a product of the subconscious. The subconscious includes extrasensory perception. Nightmares can also be triggered by present or impending events. Your mind may be warning you that something is coming. Just what that is will remain to be seen and dealt with when the time comes."

Bill was stunned. Alexandre sounded like he was a professor of some sort. "I would ask you how you have so much knowledge, but that would be insulting."

Alexandre smiled and sat back in his chair, not offering a remark.

There was a rap on the door.

Alexandre said, "Come. Come."

The door opened and there stood Emma with a plate of food.

Alexandre looked at Bill and shrugged. "I guess I'll leave you kids alone. Eat well and rest well."

CHAPTER 6

Josef Kramer stood on the east dock with his binoculars to his eyes. Spangler had no clue what he was looking for, and at this point, he really didn't care. He just wanted to be rid of the one person who was making his life even more difficult than it already was.

Kramer had slowed construction to a crawl due to his constant belittling of the workers. He screamed at the people for hours on end. He even pushed a few.

Spangler wanted that transport ship to get Kramer—and for him to never return.

Kramer handed the binoculars to Spangler. "Tell me what you see over there."

"What am I looking for?"

"Up there on the hill. Is that a church?"

"It's the old church at Ablain, or at least an offshoot of the church chain." Spangler had used the word "chain" and then wondered if that was the proper term. Maybe a diocese? He had no idea what sort of church it actually was, but he offered a comment anyway, not as a question, but as a matter of fact.

"It's a Catholic church," said Spangler confidently.

"You sound pretty sure of yourself, Spangler."

Spangler hoped that Kramer wouldn't challenge his comment by asking more questions. He could only make up so much information before the house of cards came crashing down, so he sidestepped Kramer's comment.

Spangler viewed the church through the binoculars. "I see movement off to the left. It looks like three farmers."

Kramer smiled. "Yes. We apparently didn't crush their will enough to make them want to be dead." His smile quickly disappeared. "That's a shame. I'll eventually have to correct that mistake. For now, we've got bigger fish to fry."

Emma was on her perch, which was unusual for that time of day, but she wanted to digest the experiences she'd faced over the past few days. A young man had been brought into the home and welcomed with open arms. He was personable, kind, and somewhat meek. Emma was in denial. She had unexplained feelings rising to the surface, and that was not what she wanted to happen. She didn't even know where to begin to define the feelings. She hadn't expected to ever meet another man again, and now a man had been presented to her all but wrapped up in a bow.

Emma gazed out over the ashes of the city and then to the dock facilities. Her gaze shifted to the east dock where she saw two men looking at the church with binoculars. It made her shiver. She knew what the Nazis were capable of, and she was afraid of them looking in her direction. It could only mean one thing: They were planning something devious, and it probably involved her friends and family. She hoped not.

"Emma?" her mother called out.

Emma could see her mother at the head of the stairs with her hands on her hips. She knew that her mother had been cooking; she was wearing her apron and carrying a spoon in one hand.

"I'm here, Mother," Emma said as she began the climb down from the perch.

"It's time to take food to our friend. He will probably be able to feed himself as he was able to sit up just now."

Emma would drop off the food, show her good social graces to Bill, and then be off to find her father. He needed to be made aware of what she had seen on the docks.

Emma entered the kitchen where all the ladies of the church home were busy doing the various jobs of cooking and cleaning.

Mother looked at Emma. "The plate is over there." She pointed to the counter across from the main entrance.

Emma collected the plate and could feel the warmth of the food on the bottom of it. She covered the dish with a clean cloth and then made her way to the bedroom. She rapped on the door.

"Come. Come."

Emma opened the door, and there sat Bill on his bed. Rabiah was seated next to him at the foot of the bed, and her father was seated in the chair next to the door.

Emma sat the plate on the bedside table and asked Bill, "Are you okay to feed yourself or do you need help?"

Bill looked at the plate and decided that he was okay. "I think I can do this on my own, but I would appreciate your company if it's okay with you."

Alexandre looked at Rabiah. "I think we can take a hint," he said with a wry grin.

Both men made their exit.

Emma pulled the chair by Bill's bedside and uncovered the plate.

"It looks really good, as usual," Bill said. He was always delighted by the food and Emma's company. No one could ever complain about the food in this loving church home. And Bill would never complain about the time he spent with Emma. In many ways, he had the good life here, and that was a blessing!

June 7, 1943, Polebrook, England

Henry Jenkins was dressed in his best uniform blues as he sat at lunch in the mess hall. It was the memorial service for all the bombers and the crews they had lost in battles over the last month. From his rear turret gunner position, Henry had not been able to keep an eye on Bill since Bill's plane had been one of the leaders in the formation.

Henry tapped on the lip of his coffee cup as he remembered recent battles. He had seen the deaths of men he had befriended. Bill was a good friend, and Henry felt dejected when the reports showed that he was MIA and possibly KIA. He'd heard tales of men who were presumed dead who were actually alive and either captured or hiding in towns or forests. Henry hoped Bill had survived.

Breaking away from deep thoughts, Henry looked at his watch and determined that it was time to get to the service. He put his coffee cup in the tray on the counter and made his way out the door, to the left and down the long driveway to the main office area. As he was passing the garage, he met up with one of his newest friends who seemed perplexed.

"Hello, Calvin."

"Hiya, Henry. I seem to be lost. I've only been here a couple of days, and I'm having a hard time finding stuff."

Calvin Harmon had joined the 351st just a couple of days earlier and was part of Henry's bomb crew on the 507th Squadron. He was assigned as the bombardier on the plane, and he was very competent at his job. Henry had been impressed with the accuracy of his drops.

Henry and Calvin continued their walk to the main office and discussed this and that about the mission they had flown together. There were some happy thoughts and some not-so-happy thoughts.

When they arrived at the memorial service, the place was jam-packed with the crews from all the planes. There were officials there who had traveled from the United States, and even some British officials were in attendance. Henry counted twenty chairs on the main stage. The men in them were highly decorated with medals and color bars. It was a solemn sight, and Henry was awed by the silence for the reverence of the dead and missing airmen.

After the service, Henry returned to the barracks. He thought about all the missing crew members lost in action. Could some of them be alive? This thought would haunt Henry for a long time to come.

CHAPTER 7

Emma left the bedroom with the empty plate and took it back to the kitchen. Alexandre was at the table and smiled at her as she passed. Emma put the plate in the sink and returned to her father. "If you have a few minutes, I need to speak with you, Father."

"Of course, child. I always have time for you."

"I saw something on the east dock that disturbed me, and I thought you should know about it."

"Oh?" said her father with a furrowed brow. "What did you see?"

Emma drew in a deep breath and then exhaled. It was disturbing enough to have to look at the Nazis, but it was even more disturbing to have to talk about them. Emma pulled a chair closer to her father and sat down. "I saw two men. They took turns with binoculars, and they were looking at the church. One of the men was dressed like the man I saw the night the city was ... destroyed."

Alexandre sat in silence for a few moments. This news was indeed disturbing, and he was trying to wrap his head around the situation.

"And you're sure the one man was the same?"

"Yes, Father. I am sure of that."

Emma looked at the floor and was almost sick to the point of vomiting at having had to both see and talk about the Nazis. Alexandre stood up and kissed Emma on the top of the head. "It's okay, child. This will be taken care of."

Emma had no idea what that meant, but she knew that her father would not fail in doing exactly what he said he would do.

There was a squeak of a door behind her, and she turned in her chair to see Bill standing in the doorway.

"Mind if I join you?" Bill grunted as he struggled to stand.

Emma was truly horrified. She stood up and ran to Bill. "We've got to get you back to bed!" she exclaimed, almost in tears.

Emma put her hands around his waist, and he put his arm over her shoulder.

Grunting and struggling, they finally made it to the bed.

Bill sat, and he and Emma came face-to-face. They were literally nose to nose.

After a few moments, Emma took her arms from around Bill. He reluctantly removed his arm from her shoulder. "Amazing what a man has got to do to get a hug around here."

"You did that for a hug?" Emma asked, smiling, even though she hadn't meant to smile.

"I was only joking, but the hug was very nice," Bill said softly. Bill was fighting the urge to kiss her.

Emma wanted to be kissed, and she was contemplating making the first move.

Almost involuntarily, their lips moved closer together very slowly. They closed their eyes in anticipation of that first kiss. She put her hands on his shoulders, and he put his hands on her waist. They felt the intense electricity in the air.

The moment was interrupted by a knock at the door.

Emma backed away from Bill in fear of being caught in a compromising position.

Bill took his hands off her waist.

"Come. Come," Bill said.

The door opened, and Alexandre popped his head in. Seeing Emma there, he asked, "Am I interrupting anything?"

"No, Father," Emma said. "Bill got out of bed, and I helped him back in."

Emma had turned a very deep shade of red.

Noticing her embarrassment, Bill cleared this throat and said, "You had a tough time helping me. Why don't you go outside and get some fresh air?"

Emma nodded and made her exit.

Alexandre watched her leave. He looked back at Bill with a smile, and his eyes slanted. Alexandre was not a stupid man, and it was possible that he knew a thing or two about courtship.

Bill cleared his throat again. "What can I do for you, Alexandre?"

Alexandre sat in the chair and folded his arms across his chest. He smiled and said, "Emma has been happier since you've been here."

"It's been really nice having her to help me, sir."

Bill felt the need to use the word "sir" in case Alexandre had intentions of scolding him amid the musing. Alexandre unfolded his arms and shifted in his chair. "Emma told me something that's very disturbing." Bill couldn't imagine what that could be.

"She told me that there are Nazi officers watching us. I figured I would discuss this with you before I took it before the other men of the home."

"That can't be good. How often?"

"When the city was attacked two years ago and just this afternoon. They had binoculars and were watching us."

"I have to get off this bed."

"You need to get well. Getting off the bed is the goal, but we don't need to rush anything."

"There's one other thing," continued Alexandre. "On the day you arrived, we saw a plume of smoke on the next rise over, about two miles away. Is it possible that it was a bomber crashing?"

Bill pondered this question for a moment.

"Might be worth checking it out."

"I'll get with the other men, and we'll include you in the conversation," Alexandre said. "We'll discuss the Nazis and the crashed plane."

Bill felt blessed knowing that he was being treated like family in many ways. These were good people … and good people were what he needed.

Emma was on her perch for the second time that day. It wasn't even dark, and yet she had come here to think. Again! She was falling for Bill. She hoped that he was falling for her. It was too late for her to put up her defenses since he was already in her heart. That near kiss was just like a real kiss to her. The interruption was disappointing, but she knew there would be a next time. Maybe next time there wouldn't be any interruptions.

Her mind was going in a million directions at this point. She wanted to be next to Bill and share his every thought and every experience. A big smile was on her face, and she couldn't erase it. Not that she wanted it to go away. There were very few times that she had smiled in the past two years, and now it felt good to be able to smile without trying. Just knowing that she was falling for Bill was both scary and exciting at the same time. What if he didn't love her too? She longed for the next time she would see him.

CHAPTER 8

The hall was long and well lit, and as luck would have it, James Mason and his partner, Miles Poindexter, had to walk the full length.

"I'm really nervous," said Miles as he wiped a bead of sweat off his forehead.

"I know, Miles. You've told me that over and over."

"I can't help it! I've got a nervous stomach," Miles said.

Jim rolled his eyes.

"How much farther, Jim? You know I tire out easily!"

"Hush, Miles. You're on my nerves! I don't know why they sent you with me. I guess the OSS has a very dry sense of humor." Jim shot a sideways glance at Miles.

"What do you mean by that? I'm qualified to do this job!"

"You're qualified to get on my nerves. Now shut up!"

Miles was not qualified to be a OSS operative, but the Bureau had required the presence of two operatives to be present at major presentations.

They had reached the end of the hall. Suite 162 was the office of Edward P. Davies, the director of the MI6 Information Division in London, England.

Jim paused outside the door to collect his thoughts. He adjusted his tie and entered the office. Jim, with Miles in tow, approached the receptionist. Jim said, "Would you please tell Mr. Davies that James Mason and Miles Poindexter from the OSS are here to see him?"

The receptionist smiled and nodded and then picked up the phone.

Miles was still complaining about this and that, and Jim was still rolling his eyes and wishing that he had been given a different partner.

"Mr. Davies will see you now, gentlemen. I'll buzz you in."

The office was impressive to say the least. Portraits lined the walls and there were awards up the ying-yang.

"Hey, Ed. It's good to see you!" Jim said with a big smile.

"Hey, Ed," said Miles as he offered his hand.

Mr. Davies just looked at Miles with his hands on his hips. He shot a glance over to Jim, and Jim looked at the floor and shook his head. "You will refer to this man as Mr. Director!" retorted Jim.

"Oh, sorry," said Miles. "I heard you call him Ed, so I thought it was okay."

"Don't do as I do. Do as I say!" growled Jim.

The director shook hands with Jim while glaring at Miles.

"Have a seat," said Davies. "I already know why you're here."

"Good. We can cut to the chase then. We've got an ongoing issue at Saint-Nazaire, France. The ship dry docks are controlled by the Germans. But, of course, you already knew this."

"Yes, I did. We've been painfully aware of the situation here at the agency for quite some time. What I don't understand is exactly what you're proposing," Davies said as he wrinkled his face in puzzlement.

"If you'll bear with me for a few minutes, I'll lay out a plan that I hope you'll get on board with. We need to get your approval because you have close ties with Prime Minister Churchill, and he'll have the final vote on whether to accept or deny the request."

"I'm listening," Davies said. "My mind is open."

Jim said, "We've got an inside contact at Saint-Nazaire. He can arrange to get us in and out with minimal casualties."

"And who is this contact?" By this time, the director was on the edge of his seat, leaning his elbows on his desk.

"Lieutenant Adelbert Spangler."

"You've got to be kidding me! He's part of the SS and the Nazi Party!" Davies was visibly shaken by the news.

"Yes. We're aware of all this, but he's fed us information in the past that has helped us tremendously. If you want a list of the ships that have been sunk due to his efforts, I'll be glad to supply that information to you."

"I'm simply dumbfounded. I was unaware that any Nazi was a turncoat." The director leaned back in his chair in contemplation. It was simply too much information to process all at once. They now had an inside operative, and it turned out to be someone who the director had targeted for death on his high-target list. He was angry! Jim had withheld this information from him—and after forty years of friendship!

The director's face was red, and he pounded his fist on his desk. "Why did you withhold this information from me, Jim?"

Miles wiped his face again and fidgeted in his chair. Jim looked at Miles.

"Now's the time for you to leave. Get out of here. Wait for me in the waiting room."

"S … s … sure," stammered Miles as he got up and ran for the door.

Jim looked calmly at Davies. Davies then softened up enough to listen to the explanation with less anger.

"Two words, old friend. Plausible deniability! Someone in the upper chain of command had to be oblivious to the fact that there was a spy in the mix. You were the obvious choice because of your position. Great Britain is in the part of the world that is in the middle of the war, and you have to be tough and rule with an iron fist. We needed someone to delegate authority to his operatives without pulling punches. If you had known before now that Spangler was spilling secrets, would you have been able to keep the man on a death list? It would have raised suspicions from many of the wrong people on multiple levels."

Ed leaned back in his chair as if he were exhausted.

"Thank you for being honest with me, Jim. This proposal you sent makes a lot more sense now."

Jim said, "We've got to get a team in there soon! It has to be a covert operation! No two ways about it! Only the best of the best!"

Ed took a long look at his old friend and then reached for the candy bowl on his desk. He took out a piece of candy and offered some to Jim. "I'll pass this proposal on to the proper hands."

It had just become dusk, and Emma was on her perch for the final time that day. A mild, warm breeze was blowing on her face and she was comfortable. She hadn't been this comfortable in a long time. Her thoughts raced among several things, but only one thought was in the forefront of all others.

"Emma?"

Emma recognized the voice, and it startled her. She looked down the makeshift staircase and saw Bill standing at the head of the stairs from the crypt. She was both happy and concerned all at once.

"What are you doing out of bed?"

"Your father fashioned a crutch out of a tree limb, and I decided to try it."

"You look like you're pretty steady with the crutch."

"I don't even think I need the crutch," Bill said as he playfully pretended to throw the limb away.

"No. Let's not be bold. Men are always trying to show their toughness," Emma said in a sarcastic voice as she rolled her eyes.

They both laughed, and then Bill said in the sexiest and deepest voice that he could possibly muster,

"May I join you, milady?"

Emma giggled like a schoolgirl. "It may not be a good idea to have you climb these stairs. Some of the stones are loose and may shift."

"I'll take my chances."

"If I can't talk you out of it, then I'll help you."

Bill had already started to climb. He was on the third step when Emma got down to him. She cradled his right arm with her left arm, and they made it to the top. They sat down on the stone bench and were silent for a moment. Bill surveyed his surroundings and thought that they made a pretty good place to hide and to think. To his right was the wall of the church. A short wall surrounded the platform on the other three sides, and there was a bench that they were sitting on. There was no roof, so one could see the stars above. This was the perfect place to be, and Bill could understand why Emma had selected it as her place of solitude.

Bill noticed that Emma was still holding his arm. She was looking at him with a smile.

Bill smiled at her and took her by the hand. He then reached over with his left hand and put it on the other side of her hand until it was completely surrounded. Her smile had become a look of contemplation and expectation. She pursed her lips involuntarily. Bill felt as though a gravitational pull had caused him to move his face toward hers. Their lips touched. The kiss seemed to last only a few seconds, but in reality, it lasted at least a minute. Emma put her right hand on Bill's left cheek. The kiss ended as Bill moved a few inches from her lips. Emma still had her eyes closed as she let out a long sigh. Bill leaned back against the wall and put his arm around her. Emma leaned against his chest, and they were silent. They just watched the stars together. They were both satisfied, and no one had interrupted them.

CHAPTER 9

Bill was woken by the low-key chatter outside the bedroom door, and he got up to investigate.

He opened the door, and there were all the men of the church home sitting and drinking coffee and carrying on a bit of small talk.

Alexandre looked up and saw Bill. "Ah. You're awake. Must have had a long night?"

"I got to bed late," Bill said.

"We saved you a seat," Alexandre said as he motioned to a chair.

Bill sat, and one of the ladies in the kitchen brought him a cup of coffee. The room became quiet, and a solemn feeling surrounded the group.

"I was told that we were being watched by the Nazis," began Alexandre. He paused as he thought carefully about his next words.

"We can't chance any trouble, so I suggest here and now that we make preparations to move the women and children."

All the men looked down at the table, seemingly in deep thought.

Bill looked at Alexandre and said, "A Nazi operation as large as what we've seen here is bound to have caught the attention of the Allies. I have no doubt in my mind that they will deal with the problem at hand. The Americans and the British both have spy planes, and you have to know that they've taken pictures of the docks here. Neither of these powers is going to allow this ship-repair operation to happen for very long."

Alexandre and the other men looked at each other and then looked at Bill.

"I suppose you're right," Alexandre said, "but it will still be on the safe side to prepare for an escape … just in case."

The other men nodded in approval. Bill hoped that he had been right in what he had said. Otherwise, the lives of all these people were in his hands. Now he wished that he hadn't made a comment at all.

Alexandre said, "The second article of business is the plume of smoke we saw up on the ridge. Maybe we should have investigated it shortly after it happened, but better late than never, I suppose."

The ridge to which Alexandre was referring was an area that was not really ever patrolled by the Nazi infantry. It wasn't near the water, so it wasn't a big concern to the operation of the docks.

After Alexandre had made his suggestion, there was a vote. All agreed to do the investigation.

"We'll have to do it at night. We need not all go, so we need to decide who will be on the team. Maybe three? I'll be the first to volunteer," Alexandre said as he raised his hand.

Bill raised his hand as well.

"You may need a doctor—even if I'm only a horse doctor." Rabiah smiled.

The group chuckled.

"Then it's settled. We'll leave at dusk."

Emma was in the kitchen with her mother and the other ladies and had heard the conversation.

Josephine looked at Emma and knew what she was thinking. "Concern for your man is natural. You'll learn to deal with it."

Emma nodded.

Bill limped up the stairs and out onto the ruins. He saw a fairly large hole in the outer wall and pulled up a stone to sit on. Gazing out, he could clearly see the docks and all the busy activity going on.

Suddenly he felt a pair of hands on the side of his head. The fingers slid around his ears and covered his eyes.

"Guess who?"

"Um … the tooth fairy?"

"No!" Emma laughed and removed her hands from Bill's face. She gave him a quick kiss and moved around to sit between his knees.

Bill softly massaged her shoulders, and she tilted her head back from the sheer pleasure. Bill gave her an upside-down kiss.

"Is that all I get?" asked Emma sarcastically.

"Well, it's daylight, and we are in full view of other people," Bill said.

The conversation paused for several seconds. Emma reached to her shoulders and took Bill by both hands. She looked down at her feet and fell into deep concentration.

Bill sensed that there was something on her mind and decided to break the silence.

"Is something bothering you, dear?"

Emma hesitated. She was unsure how to answer.

"I heard your conversation with the other men," answered Emma.

"And I'm guessing that it bothered you in some way?"

"Yes. It bothered me greatly."

There was a moment of silence. Bill contemplated the absolute correct way to calm the fears of his new love. He didn't want her to worry, and he knew that he had to do what was necessary to help protect all the families in the church home. The plane was loaded with 1,700 gallons of fuel and had used about 700 before it was shot down. A thousand gallons of fuel would be useful as a weapon in a pinch. However, he realized that he was being presumptuous. Maybe it wasn't a bomber at all. It could be an FW-190.

"What we're about to do is for the benefit of the family," Bill whispered in her ear.

Emma stood straight up and sat on Bill's lap. She wrapped her arms around him and put her chin on his shoulder as she looked up at the next rise. She was concerned, but she also understood the importance of what Bill was trying to accomplish. All that was left to do was for her to convince herself that it was all going to be all right.

Emma whispered in Bill's ear, "I know."

London

"Hello, Edward," grumbled the large man chewing a cigar. "To what do I owe this pleasure?"

Director Edward Davies had been standing outside the prime minister's door, waiting on him to return. Sir Winston Churchill was having a bit of trouble with the lock on his office door.

"Confounded lock!" grumbled Churchill.

"The pleasure is all mine, Mr. Prime Minister."

The lock finally freed and the door was open.

"Well? Are you coming in or not?"

"Sorry, sir. I guess I was waiting on an invitation."

"I see you've brought your briefcase with you—so this won't be a social visit?"

"I'm afraid not, sir. I've got desperately important business to discuss with you."

"Then share it with me. I don't have all day, Edward!"

Director Davies spent the next few minutes describing the necessity for a commando intervention in Saint-Nazaire and showed him facts and figures on paper. They would need twenty-five commandos from the UK and twenty-five from the US.

"This will be a covert operation, sir. Choosing the men and training them will take approximately two months to complete."

"Are you looking for a rubber stamp, Edward?"

"No, sir. But expedience is needed. The docks will be complete in six months, according to spy plane images. And after that, U-boats will be all over the map."

The plan that Jim Mason had sent to Edward showed the need for fifty total commandos. The fact that they had a Nazi lieutenant in the bag was a good thing, and he would prove to be very useful. The Nazi dock soldiers would be shifted around to accommodate the movement of the commandos. Large amounts of explosives would be used to detonate under the foundation of the docks. The reason for the lower-level explosives was that the Nazis were trying hard to protect the roofs of the buildings from bombers. They would never expect an attack at ground level since the compound was patrolled very tightly by many sentries. Therefore, the foundations were not constructed as well as the other parts of the buildings.

"The commandos would have to be good swimmers since most of the operation would be underwater. An RDX composition-C explosive would be used in high quantities. It is a very destructive explosive and would level one square mile with a ten-pound load."

Churchill said, "Very impressive plan, Edward!"

"Yes, sir. I thought so myself."

"Go ahead and start training. I'll get this to Parliament for final approval."

"Yes, sir."

Night had fallen, and Bill awaited the time for the mission. The mission? Didn't his last mission end in disaster? What would they find at the crash site? Too many questions needed to be answered, and Bill was ready for the answers!

Bill stepped out of the bedroom to meet them.

"Are we ready to go?"

"We're ready when you are," Alexandre said.

Rabiah nodded his head.

The walk was made in silence in case they attracted Nazi attention. Bill put his finger to his lips to signal to the other two that they needed to maintain this air of silence.

The walk took about forty-five minutes before they arrived at the site where they had seen the plume of smoke. Several trees had been sheered down to the stumps, and there were drag marks and several shallow trenches for about two hundred yards. Off a short distance it appeared that there was a clump of trees that were strangely close together as if they had been knocked over and placed as such.

Alexandre looked at Bill and quietly asked, "What does this look like to you?"

"It looks like a plane crashed."

"And it looks like it may have been a large one."

They walked for a distance toward the clump of trees. Within the clump was a glimmering shape. A new moon was at its zenith, and whatever was in the tree line glimmered from its light. They continued to walk toward the tree line.

Bill had expected to see some debris from the crash, but there was none.

As they reached the tree line, Bill pulled back a few branches. Treetops were on the ground, and the bottoms were in the air. The three men tunneled through the overturned trees for about twenty feet before reaching a wall of metal.

Alexandre lit the lantern and held it close. It was a sight that was all too familiar to Bill. It was a B-17G bomber.

They moved along the length of the metal sheet and found a hole in the wall, which they slowly and carefully slipped through. The silence was absolutely deafening. The plane was like a ghost town.

Bill looked down at the walkway from the cockpit to as far as he could see to the back. There was a bloody mark along the length. Bill moved toward the cockpit, slipped between the bombs in the bomb chutes, and made it to the pilots' box above the right-side window. He opened it and found a flashlight and a pair of binoculars.

He returned to the bomb chutes and shined the flashlight up and down the bombs and to the ground below the bomb bay.

There were six, thousand-pound high-explosive bombs still intact. The frame holding the bombs was worse for wear, but the bombs appeared to be in good shape. The drop chutes in the bay were heavily damaged, and there were burn marks all over the bay where the 88-millimeter shell had done its damage.

The pungent odor of death was in the air. A decaying body was somewhere nearby.

The three men walked toward the rear of the plane. They found a few flashlights in the utility boxes that were along the top of the wall in the radio officer's area. They worked. These flashlights were designed for military use. They had a dial over the bulb to change the color to red, and a setting for dim light.

"These flashlights will come in handy," Bill said. "Follow me and stay close."

The smell of rotting flesh had become intense, so the men pulled their shirt collars up to cover the lower parts of their faces.

They continued to move to the back of the plane, and they came within sight of the waist gunner's station. Bill spotted what appeared to be a human shape. Its face was against the wall at the left gunner's rack. Bill reached down and rolled over the body. The body was badly decomposed, and Bill could only surmise it was Sam. The plane that had crashed here was indeed the plane that had almost been his death trap.

Bill took a moment to pay respect to his fallen friend and crew mate.

Alexandre and Rabiah took off their hats and bowed their heads. There would certainly have to be a proper burial later.

Bill shined his flashlight out through the waist gunner's window and noticed that the trees on the left side were standing upright. He surmised that the plane had hit the ground and spun in a 360-degree angle and had sheared off the right wing, which became trapped under the plane. The nose had hit the first line of trees and uprooted them, turning the plane an extra ninety degrees in the same direction as the first turn. The plane came to rest with the trees shaped like a tent over the framework. It was a nearly perfect hiding place. The fuselage was badly damaged and very bent, but it was still pretty much intact.

Bill checked the waist guns and found that the left gun was too badly damaged to salvage. The ammo belt was in good shape, but the gun had been hit by enemy fire, and the base of the gun rack had seen better days. The right gun was amazingly intact, but still needed some repairs.

The men picked up Sam's body and moved back toward the hole in the wall where they had initially entered. Bill stepped out, and Alexandre and Rabiah handed the body through the hole, slowly and carefully. They moved his body a short distance to one of the trenches dug by the broken wing and laid him to rest there. They moved the loose soil over the body, and each said their own words over the makeshift grave. They didn't have any shovels, so they would have to come back later to perform a proper burial.

The men set their flashlights on dim and started their journey back to the church home. They walked in total silence as each of them were in some way changed by what they had seen. Alexandre and Rabiah had seen a weapon of death, and Bill had seen his friend as a decayed reminder of what the ravages of war could do to the ability to interact with that friend.

Josephine and Emma were seated at the big dining room table and sipping on coffee. Emma was deep in thought and totally motionless. She stared at her coffee cup with a worried look on her face.

Emma's mother was hesitant to interrupt her train of thought, so she did as she had known Emma's father to do in times like these and waited for the right time to make a comment. She didn't like to see Emma suffer, but she wanted to make sure that she wasn't intruding on her inner thoughts.

Josephine drew in a breath and said "Emma?"

Emma was unmoving and apparently either didn't hear her mother or was too engrossed in her thoughts to notice that her name had been called.

Josephine again drew a breath and spoke a little louder. "Emma?"

Emma shuddered as she was brought back from the land of thought and into the land of reality. She had been unaware that she had tunneled so deeply into her personal thoughts that her coffee had gone cold.

"Yes, Mother?"

Josephine smiled at Emma to try to help calm her fears.

"I'm concerned for your father—just as you are concerned for Bill. I also know that it's a man's place to protect his family. What these men are doing is investigating a situation that may lead to our protection. They are willing to take risks to make sure this happens."

Emma thought about this explanation. Her mother was right, and maybe Emma needed to be more understanding. Bill had risked his life on that plane on the bombing raid—not only to protect his own country but also to protect her life and the lives of the French people. "I can't help but feel the way I feel, Mother."

"I know. After the many times your father took on the responsibilities he has over the years, I've learned to take the facts as they come. No one ever said life was going to be easy."

Emma was ashamed that she had been so selfish, and she drooped her shoulders.

Josephine picked up on this change, and she leaned forward to pat Emma on the shoulder.

As she stood up, the men returned. Alexandre was first, then Bill, and Rabiah was last. Emma bolted out of her chair and ran to Bill. She put her arms around him and put her head on his chest. With the sheer relief that he was returned to her safe and sound, she began to weep.

Alexandre opened his mouth to try to calm her, but Josephine signaled to him with her hand to leave her alone.

Alexandre and Rabiah left the room to leave the three others in peace.

Bill was unsure of what was happening and was genuinely concerned. "What's wrong, Emma?" Bill said.

"Just shut up and hold me!"

CHAPTER 10

Henry stepped into the main office building and found the office of Colonel Marcus Windsor, the commanding officer for the base. The door was open, and Henry knocked on the frame.

Colonel Windsor was on the phone and motioned for Henry to enter.

"Sergeant Henry Jenkins reporting. You wanted to see me, sir?"

"At ease. At ease," said the colonel, flopping his hand in the air as if he were telling Henry to dispense with the formalities. "Have a seat, airman."

Henry had no idea what the colonel wanted to discuss with him, and he was very nervous. People weren't usually called into the office to have cake and ice cream. It was usually a bad thing.

The colonel looked Henry over as if he were trying to decide something. Henry shifted in his seat nervously.

After what seemed like an eternity, the colonel finally spoke. "I've received an order from that pushy bunch of bureaucrats upstairs. I need to get a couple of men together to train for something big."

"I see, sir. And you chose me?"

"That would be the reason I brought you in here today."

"I'll do whatever you need, sir."

"Good." The colonel got off his chair and walked to the door and closed it. He returned to his seat, took a sheet of paper off his desk, and handed it to Henry. Henry took the paper and saw that it was a document from the State Department.

"They're impressed with your work, son. You've been on eighteen missions in six weeks with no injuries. You've protected the tail end of your aircraft with precision shots, and you seem fearless. That sort of thing does not go unnoticed!"

Henry took a second to look up from the paper at the colonel. "Thank you, sir!"

Henry was surprised to see the name of the city as the center of attention for the need of commando involvement: Saint-Nazaire. Three crews had been lost on that bombing raid, along with his friend Bill McLaughton. It had been a hard-fought battle, and he certainly hoped that his friend had survived. "I like what I see here, sir, I'd like to accept the offer."

"Good. We'll draw up the paperwork and get you on your way."

Bill and Emma were seated on the perch. Bill was looking through his binoculars at the docks. A large ship had pulled into the east dock and was unloading a frail-looking bunch of people. It seemed to Bill that they were being herded like cattle. "Those are Jews," Bill said as he handed the binoculars to Emma.

"How do I use this … thing?"

"Put them to your eyes and use the knob in the center to focus."

"You probably think I'm stupid because I don't know how to use them."

"There's nothing stupid about people not knowing how to do things." Bill folded his arms across his chest as he thought of a way to explain to Emma the difference between smart and stupid. "You know how to cook, right?"

"Yes. I've been cooking since I was a young girl."

"Well, I don't know how to cook. I guess that makes me stupid."

"Lots of people don't know how to cook, silly man!"

"Lots of people don't know how to use military equipment. Does that make them stupid? Does that make me smart?"

"Okay. I see your point," Emma said as she finally figured out how to make the confusing contraption work. She gasped. She had never seen human bodies in such bad shape—and so very frail and skinny. They all staggered along as if they didn't have enough strength to move without being prodded.

Angry soldiers were pushing, shoving, and shouting at the people. Some of them were even hit with the butts of the rifles.

Emma closed her eyes and abruptly handed the binoculars to Bill. She choked back a sob and sunk her head to her chest.

Bill put his arms around her and pulled her close, tucking her head to his chest.

"Why is this happening?" asked Emma after a long pause.

Bill thought deeply on the question. He didn't have an answer, but he would certainly try to give the best possible interpretation. "Nazis think of themselves as a master race. They view Jews as being inferior. Jews, to them, are basically animals."

"It's the Nazis who are the animals," Emma said, trying desperately to choke back the tears. She didn't want to cry. She had cried to Bill on many occasions, but she didn't want to become someone who had nothing but tears to offer. Bill kissed the top of her head. "Let it all out. I'm here for you."

Washington, DC

Jim entered his office at the Pentagon and set his coffee on the desk. It was going to be a long day, and he was not looking forward to meeting with the Joint Chiefs. He'd been in the War Room before, and the looks he got from the higher-ups were less than flattering. On the other hand, the military personnel that staffed the offices beneath the Joint Chiefs were always friendly to him. He had a history with all but a few of them, and they always greeted him with a smile and a handshake.

Jim was jolted out of his thoughts. His phone had started ringing. "Jim Mason," he said in his most professional voice.

"Hey, Jim. It's Ed."

"Well, a friendly voice for once today."

"Yeah. I know you're going into the War Room soon," Ed said. "Just thought I'd let you know that the plan has been approved."

"A friendly voice and good news? At least my day is starting off well."

"We've got a group of twenty-five together, and they'll start training in three days. We've got a group of highly talented men."

"That's a good thing, Ed. We've got twenty-five of our finest. I guess it would be best to suggest to the Joint Chiefs that we train the teams together."

"That would be a good idea. We've got a facility in Bermuda."

"Talk soon, Ed." As Jim hung up the phone, he realized that the plans he had helped make were going to be approved by all teams. He was suddenly aware of the nagging responsibility that if the mission failed, he would hold himself responsible for the deaths of all those men. This feeling didn't sit well with him.

The phone in his office started ringing again, and he was once again shaken loose from his thoughts.

"Jim Mason."

"The Joint Chiefs will see you now, sir," his secretary said.

"Thank you, Julie. Please let them know that I'm on my way."

The walk down to the first floor wasn't all that much of a distance. The Pentagon is huge, but the way Jim's office was situated, it was directly above the War Room. It was a short walk down the hallway to the ramp and then a quick right into the door that housed the place where most of the plans for war were made.

Jim entered the room about five minutes before the session was due to start. Some familiar faces were around the tables, and he nodded and spoke to a few. Jim found the place that had been set aside for him from the tab on the front of the table marked "Mr. Mason." He felt official. The Joint Chiefs may not see him as official, but the nameplate made him feel like he was.

The speaker stood behind the podium and tapped his gavel, and the room became quiet. There was a large map on the wall behind the podium, and many spots were marked as to the location of ships and troops.

The Joint Chiefs took their seats on the podium. The seating area for them was like a courtroom. The bench was a full extension around one side of the room, and the Joint Chiefs were seated behind the counter. Each one of these men had a nameplate in front of where they were seated.

The chairman called for first business, and the clerk announced, "The first business on the docket is a military strategy for Saint-Nazaire, France."

"And who will present?" the chairman asked.

"Mr. Jim Mason of the OSS," the clerk said.

"Mr. Mason, nice to see you again. What do you have for us?"

Jim cleared his throat. He had already gathered the papers from his briefcase and had stacked them neatly in two piles in front of him. The first copy was his, and the second copy was for the Joint Chiefs.

"I have a copy of my proposal for you, Mr. Chairman."

"Well, don't be shy, Mr. Mason. Send it to me."

A very well-dressed young man presented himself to Jim, and Jim handed the papers to him. The papers were immediately delivered to the chairman who then put on his reading glasses but still squinted at the print.

Jim said, "We're in the process of putting together a team of commandos from the United States and the British Empire. We believe that expedience is in the best interest of the Allies."

The chairman said, "I've read the preliminary report, but it seems that this report is much more comprehensive, Mr. Mason."

"We've had a team working night and day, sir."

"Very impressive indeed. Care to elaborate on the highlights?"

"Yes, sir," Jim said. "We plan to train the commandos at a British base in Bermuda. It's remote and won't attract attention from those who wish to see operations such as this fail."

All eyes in the room were on Jim. Even those who had been looking down at their own notes were suddenly interested in what Jim had to say.

Jim said, "After training, we'll ship them to Vannes, France. We'll achieve this in shifts—five men per shipment. With a one-day space between shipments, it will take ten days to get all the men to Vannes." Jim was on a roll. He had every eye on him and every ear was soaking up what he had to say.

"The distance between Vannes and Saint-Nazaire is 89.4 kilometers—or 55.5 miles for those of you who don't like metric."

There was a small amount of laughter.

Jim said, "The team will not regroup together but will break off into camps around the area of the Ablain church ruins. Bearing in mind that spy planes have recorded that there is a bit of land there that has been farmed, there is evidence that there are people living there. These people are probably former residents of the town who were driven away by the Nazi bombing back in 1941. With this in mind, we'll have to send the first detail to speak with the residents. The commandos will each be loaded with a small amount of RDX composition plastic, which is highly explosive. We have the help of a turncoat Nazi lieutenant to help us shift the guards around to accommodate the movement of the commandos in and around the area."

There was an audible gasp in the room.

There was a question from one of the members of the Joint Chiefs. General Norman Hinckley said, "How will the commandos be transported undetected?"

"Good question, General. We've employed the help of several German spies who have either defected or who disagree with the Third Reich. We call this program Double Cross. We even have German spies who have come to us. We didn't have to go looking for them. These double agents will feed intelligence to the Nazis, which will cause them to think the ships transporting the commandos are cargo ships. The commandos will be disguised to complete the ruse. We've even fixed them up with fake identities, and we'll be able to track the progress and the pattern of the enemy surrounding the situation."

General Hinckley was satisfied with the answer, and he nodded his approval.

Jim looked around the room and said, "Are there any more questions before I continue?"

No one spoke.

Jim said, "Once the first crew of commandos reaches Vannes, they will make their way to Saint-Nazaire. There is a bus that will get within eight miles of the city before it has to turn around. Eight miles to walk is nothing for these guys. They're tough and can make that in two to three hours. Once they get to the outskirts of the city, they will attempt to contact the residents who are in the church ruins. Apparently, these people have made it two years living here, so they've got to have an organization happening there. They seem to be doing well, according to spy-plane snapshots."

Jim turned the page. "Once contact has been established with the residents, they will be advised of the situation, moved out of the church, and temporarily sheltered a few miles back up toward Vannes. Nine days later we will make a strike, and that strike will occur as follows: On the night of the raid, on a date that is not yet determined, fifteen commandos will make their way to a place two miles north of the east dock. There they will move west to a cove at a specified coordinate where there will be rubber suits used in diving, with oxygen tanks and masks. They will swim 1.3 miles back to the east dock and split up. Each commando will place ten pounds of RDX at a predetermined location. They will swim back and give the next crew the diving equipment. The process will continue until one hundred and fifty pounds of RDX have been installed at the proper locations. The remaining five commandos will man the lookout points."

Jim looked up and there was dead silence. A few moments went by, and suddenly there were a buzz of questions from different members of the panel and from the audience.

The chairman smiled. Jim knew that he had done his job.

CHAPTER 11

Henry stepped off the plane in Bermuda with his duffel bag and took a good sniff of the clean air. There was something about not having to smell the exhaust fumes of 91-octane fuel that was nice for a change. The base at Bermuda was in a lull as far as training went, and there was plenty of room available for all fifty commandos. He was glad to be away from the smell of death, but he was sorry to leave his friends behind. He wanted to be able to help protect them, and he knew that this mission was a key in taking down the bad guys. It was time to get down to brass tacks and earn his keep.

The nightmare was always the same. Bill woke up in his usual sweat, and he was panting. He glanced at his watch, and sure enough, it was 0237. There was a banging on the door, but Bill had not yet found his voice.

The door swung open, and Alexandre was standing there.

Emma pushed past him and moved quickly to the bed. She put her hands on Bill's face and swiveled it toward her. "Are you okay?"

"I'm fine. Just a nightmare."

Alexandre had stayed outside the partially closed door to give the young people some privacy.

"Come on in," Bill said.

"Thanks, Bill," Alexandre said as he grabbed the chair by the door.

"I'll go get a wet cloth and a change of bedclothes," Emma said.

Alexandre waited for Emma to leave, and then he shut the door behind her.

"Were there any additions to the nightmare?"

"There were sounds. It's like it's working toward a story."

"What did you hear?"

Bill drew in a breath and tried to remember the entire dream. "Same beginning, but now I hear a voice that says, 'Well.' I have no idea what the word means. It seems completely out of context."

Emma reentered the room with an armload of items, which she placed on the foot of the bed. She took the wet cloth, washed Bill's face, and then dried him off. She continued to wash the exposed areas on his body with great care.

"We'll talk more later. I'll leave you to recover," Alexandre said as he stood up.

Bill nodded, and Alexandre made his exit.

Emma finished changing the bed and sat down next to Bill. She took his hand and placed it to her face, kissing his knuckles. "Whatever is going on with the nightmares, I'm here to help you."

Bill put his free arm around her and kissed her lips. "I'm glad I have you to help me. I want to help you as well."

"You've done more for me than you'll ever realize," Emma whispered, trying to hold back the tears.

"I don't want you to hurt," Bill said softly, wiping the tears that pooled on her chin line.

They kissed once more.

"I want to know everything about you," Emma whispered.

"What would you like to know?"

"Tell me about your home. I'd like to know about your life."

"You already know I'm an American."

"Yes. I knew that."

"I'm from Greenfield, Indiana. Born and raised. I come from a family of farmers, but my father had to get a job in the steel industry to make ends meet."

"And you became a soldier?"

"I joined the air force when I was eighteen. I was trained as a waist gunner for the bomber group."

Emma thought for a moment and then said, "I want to see this aircraft that you and Father investigated."

"Are you sure? I'm not sure how your father would react."

"This plane brought you to me. For that, I am forever grateful. I am determined to go see this plane that brought love to me."

"Are you going to talk to your father about it?"

"I will. I'm going to tell him that I want to see it, and then explain why."

"And you think he'll agree that you need to see it?"

"I'm pretty persuasive. I'm sure he'll see it my way."

London, England

As Edward Davies entered the office, his secretary handed him a message. It was apparently an urgent communication from Jim Mason. Ed scurried to his office and picked up the phone.

"Jim Mason."

"Hello, Jim. Ed here. I got a message to call you."

"Hey, Ed. I got a communication that you should be made aware of. Lieutenant Adelbert Spangler contacted us through a secure wire and has said that the nutty General Major Josef Kramer is talking about attacking and killing the people housed in the church at Saint-Nazaire."

"How do we plan to fix this, Jim?"

"We're going to pull five members from the training camp in Bermuda to go ahead and get to Saint-Nazaire to evacuate the people from the church. If Josef Kramer attacks the church, then it may throw a few wrinkles in our plans that we don't need to iron out. We've got enough on our plate as it is."

"What actions do I need to take, Jim? I want to help out here."

"We'll pull three Americans for the new mission. Choose two of your guys. If we mix the team with members from each country, it will be better. They won't draw as much attention."

"I agree. I'll contact the Bermuda base and have them pull two of our men."

"Wish I had time to talk more, Ed. We need to get together soon. You know, for old times' sake."

"I agree, old friend. Talk later. I need to get busy too."

"There's no time to waste, Ed. We've got to move now!"

Alexandre was sitting at the table, drinking a cup of coffee, and talking to Father Ambroise and Rabiah. Mornings were always enjoyable for the men as it gave them time to catch up and to make plans for the hunting and farming jobs for the day. They liked the talks and the coffee. The conversation was always happy, and the coffee was always good.

It was just before daylight. Bill and Emma had spent the last few hours talking on the perch, and it seemed that their discussion made the time go by very quickly. They had heard the men talking and decided to go see Alexandre about Bill taking Emma to the plane. They walked down the steps into the dining area, and the three men looked up.

"Well, good morning, you two," Father said.

The other two men nodded and smiled.

"Good morning, Father. We need to speak with you when you get a chance," Emma said.

"If it's important, then maybe we need to take it to the bedroom?"

Both Father Ambroise and Rabiah mentioned that they had duties to attend to and excused themselves.

"Well, we have this room to ourselves now," Alexandre said. "Now, what do we need to discuss?"

Bill cleared his throat and looked away nervously.

Emma looked down at her hands. The whole plan had seemed like a piece of cake until it became time to actually do the deed. Bill didn't totally understand Emma's need to see the plane, but he was willing to go along with the original plan. "I want to go see the plane that brought Bill here, Father."

Alexandre tilted his head sideways with a scowl on his face. He had not seen this coming, and he was none too happy with what he had heard. As he spoke, he shot a glance toward Bill and then back to Emma. "Whose idea was this?"

"It was mine, Father."

"I can only imagine why you would want to do this."

"I want to see the plane that brought this man to me. I can't explain it. It's just that it's important to me."

Bill took Emma's hand and smiled.

Emma looked back at her father, apparently searching for the understanding that she had always known and that he had always shown her. Alexandre appeared to be struggling with the thought. It was dangerous, and he remembered the apprehension he felt on the night that they had gone to the plane. That trip had been necessary! He found himself struggling with the idea of sending his daughter into such danger.

"And you agree with her need, young man?" Alexandre inquired.

Alexandre had never called Bill "young man." He had always called him either "Bill" or "sir." The look on Bill's face was a dead giveaway that he had been taken off guard. It was as if Alexandre had planned it to elicit a truthful response. Bill cleared his throat. "I want to do whatever makes your daughter happy, sir."

"I really don't want to send you into danger. I trust Bill. Leave me for a bit to think on this please."

Bill nodded, took Emma by the hand, and exited the dining room.

"Are you honestly considering this?" came a voice from the kitchen. It was Josephine. She never wanted to eavesdrop on any conversation, but she had heard the initial banter and couldn't tear herself away. Josephine entered the dining room carrying two cups and sat where Bill and Emma had been seated.

"I have to consider it. Do I have a choice?" Alexandre said.

By the look on his face, Alexandre was obviously tormented at the prospect of his daughter being of age to make her own choices. He had guided her as a child, and he now felt as though he were backed into a corner. If he didn't allow her to go, then she would resent him. If he allowed her to go, then it would be a signal that she was no longer under his guidance. But it needed to be made known that he wanted to guide her and not control her.

"Of course you have a choice," Josephine said as she dipped her head down in an effort to catch the eyes of her husband.

Alexandre had a look of what could only be described as pure terror. He stared at his coffee cup and didn't move a muscle.

"Then help me make the choice."

"Emma is in love with this man. She's going to do what is in her heart. If you rebel against that, she will resent you," Josephine replied. "In a couple of months, she won't be a teenager anymore. You have to be prepared. She will no longer want to be treated like a child."

Alexandre sighed and put his hand down on the table, which Josephine took and squeezed. Alexandre looked up at Josephine, and she saw a tiny tear in his right eye. Alexandre stood up, kissed Josephine on the forehead, and then made his way up the stairs. He had much work to do.

Bermuda

Henry sat in the briefing room, waiting with the other forty-nine commandos. It had been a grueling few days since his training had started, but the punishment would pay off in the end. He was convinced of this belief, and he had to remind himself daily of it. It was a lot harder than he thought it would ever be, but he had toughened up with the battles that he had seen, and now the physical torture and lack of proper sleep.

The door to the briefing room opened, and a young man dressed in battle fatigues stepped in. He immediately came to a perfectly executed parade rest and began to speak. "Lieutenant Henry Jenkins?"

Lieutenant? Since when did that happen? Last Henry had known, he was a sergeant.

"I'm *Sergeant* Henry Jenkins," Henry said, hoping that he was somehow not out of line.

"I was instructed to summon Lieutenant Henry Jenkins to the CO's office," replied the young man.

Henry stood up and followed the young soldier. A short distance down the hall was the office of the commanding officer, Colonel Ralph C. Pitz.

As Henry entered, he realized that he would not be speaking alone to the CO as there were two men dressed in fine suits seated alongside the commander.

The commander motioned to a chair. "Have a seat, Lieutenant."

"Permission to speak, sir?"

"What's on your mind?"

"There must be a mistake. I am a sergeant, sir, not a lieutenant."

"That's part of what we need to discuss."

The fact that he was being addressed as a higher rank had put Henry's mind at ease—he might not be in trouble. The two men on either side of the commander looked official, and neither of the men moved. It seemed that they didn't even blink.

"The two men you see with me here are, to my left, Agent Roger Pittman from MI6 London division, and, to my right, Agent Brent Cavanaugh from the OSS."

Henry was suddenly nervous. He had no idea why he was facing two men of such a high status in government operations from both the US and Great Britain. He was obviously hiding his apprehension very well since no one seemed to notice that he was beginning to sweat.

The colonel continued, "We've been advised by the joint commands of both of our great countries that we have a situation that needs to be dealt with. This will be a need-to-know situation, and you will need to do exactly as you are told. No questions asked. Are you following me so far?"

"Yes, Colonel."

"Furthermore, you've been promoted to lieutenant. I've personally had a look at your service records, and I have to say that I am deeply impressed. I've noticed you in the training program, and you seem to be tough. You'll follow these two gentlemen to the officers' conference room to be briefed."

"Yes, Colonel." Henry stood up and followed the men to another room down the hall. They entered the door, and Henry was amazed by the size of the room. There were coffee and doughnuts on the conference table and lighted grids all around the room that contained maps of different parts of the world. The positions of troops, ships, and planes were apparently being updated electronically.

Agent Pittman excused himself so that he could meet with the two men who had been selected from the UK to join the operation.

"Have a seat, lieutenant."

Henry took a seat but was still looking at all the gadgets in the room.

Agent Cavanaugh handed Henry a bulging manila packet that seemed to contain more than just papers.

"If you'll open your packet, we'll begin."

Henry undid the clasps at the top of the envelope and opened the flap. There was a sealed white envelope, among other things, in the packet.

Cavanaugh said, "In the white envelope, you'll find your identity. A passport and your identification. You are now Harold James Watkins. You are a US citizen on your way to visit family in England because you are concerned for their well-being."

Henry nodded, signifying that he understood.

Cavanaugh said, "Now on the big stuff. In the need-to-know category, you will need to know more than the rest of the crew since you are, in effect, in charge of them." He handed a small stack of papers to Henry. "You'll notice on page 2 that your mission, beginning now, is to board a ship here at the base docks. This ship will leave at 2330. After boarding the ship, you will sail to Plymouth, England. From there, you will take a ferry to Vannes, France. You will board a bus, and it will take you to the boundary where buses can no longer travel. This boundary is approximately eight miles from the city of Saint-Nazaire, France, in a place called Saint-Malo-de-Guersac. All the coordinates and times are listed in your itinerary on page 4. Are you with me so far?"

"I understand what you're telling me, sir."

"Good. Here comes the juicy part." Cavanaugh flipped to the next page. "You will proceed—at exactly the time listed on your schedule—to the church at the top of the hill. It's an old ruin, but several families have resided there for the past two years. It's deeply important that you evacuate these people before daylight. You will follow the instructions on the next page to secure a temporary place to live for them a few miles north of Saint-Nazaire."

Henry nodded.

Henry was dismissed from the conference room. Now was the difficult part. He, as a commander, had to get with the group of men who he would have to command. Henry entered the next conference room to meet with Agent Pittman and the two British airmen the agent had selected from his group.

"Lieutenant, have a seat," Agent Pittman said as he motioned to a chair next to him. "Gentlemen, this is Lieutenant Henry Jenkins of the United States Air Force. He will be your commander for the ground group."

The briefing continued as Henry thought of the task ahead of them. He would have a lot of reading to do on his instruction sheets before they left that night—and then a lot of reading while they were traveling. This was going to prove interesting!

Saint-Nazaire

Adelbert Spangler stood on the east dock with General Major Josef Kramer and watched the transport ship pulling into the dock.

Kramer said, "I hate to leave the operations to an incompetent such as yourself, Spangler."

"I'll try not to let you down, sir."

Kramer took the binoculars out of his bag and looked back at the church. He smiled not at the sight but at the thought of destroying it along with the last vestiges of the subhuman scum that lived in it. When he destroyed the city two years ago, he intended to leave no survivors, and the thought that anyone had survived the destruction was repulsive to him.

The ship had concluded its docking procedure and Kramer boarded. Spangler thought about how nice it would be if the ship was destroyed, with the monster on board, as it headed out to sea.

Spangler retired back to his office on the main dock. He retrieved the Enigma device that was cleverly hidden in a side panel under the desk. By this date and time, the code for Enigma had been broken by the British, unbeknownst to the German high command, the SS, or the Third

Reich. With the Enigma device, it was possible to send personal messages between individuals, and Spangler had news to convey. Unbeknownst to Spangler—and the Third Reich—the British had broken the code for Enigma.

As Spangler pondered his options for after the war was all said and done, he wondered if he would even be alive. He knew that if he was, then he would have to live far away from Germany. *The United States? Hmm.*

The Enigma came to life and started cranking out code. Spangler transcribed the code and read it back: "Crew left Bermuda. Have cove cleared in two days. Ship will arrive to drop off supplies." Spangler understood why they had left early since he was the one who had told the Allies of Kramer's plan to kill the residents of the church. Spangler smiled with the knowledge that he was going to have the chance to help save those lives.

Spangler keyed back a message: "Understood. Residents safe for now. Must speed up operations." Spangler put the machine back in its hiding place and took his place back at the window overlooking the construction floor. He folded his arms across his chest and just watched.

CHAPTER 12

After dinner, the ladies went to the kitchen to wash the dishes. The children were playing in the courtyard, and the men were relaxing and drinking coffee.

Bill and Emma retired to the perch to sit and talk.

"Nice dinner this evening, wasn't it?" Bill leaned back against the wall with his hands behind his head.

"Yes, it was. Father looked like he was in deep thought."

"I feel kind of bad that we had to put that burden on him."

"It's really not worth worrying him. I may just delay going." Emma stared at the broken concrete floor.

"Whatever makes you happy. I'll do whatever you want to do."

Alexandre approached and said, "Bill? Emma? May I come up and talk to you both?"

"Of course, Father. You're always welcome. It's not a private club." Emma rolled her eyes.

Bill and Alexandre laughed.

Alexandre made his climb and was panting as if it had been torturous.

"I'm apparently getting old." Alexandre was out of breath.

"You're just getting more refined," Bill said jokingly.

"The reason I came up here is to—"

"Let me go first, Father."

"Go ahead, child."

"Bill and I apologize for putting this kind of thing on you. I have decided to postpone the trip to the plane until another time."

Bill nodded in favor of the apology. Alexandre just looked at Emma. He was proud of her for putting his feelings ahead of her own.

"I was about to give you my blessing to go. I'll leave you two alone, and I need to stop calling you *child*. You're my grown baby. I'll start calling you *dear*."

Emma realized then and there that her father was indeed a good man. He had trusted her, and that meant the world to her. She couldn't imagine her life without her father.

Bermuda, July 19, 1943

Henry met with his team at the dock.

Sergeant Mark Banion of the US Air Force had been a turret gunner for a variety of bases, and Sergeant Peter Wolford was a bomber pilot from the US Air Force.

James Bartow and Paul Hightower were British fighter pilots.

The ship had arrived on time. It was a beauty! It was flying the American and British flags, which was a bit confusing. The base at Bermuda was a British training camp. Now, an American ship was there to pick them up to take them to England.

Henry approached the ship with his team. He'd never seen a battleship of its size. He read the name on the nose of the ship. It was the USS *Massachusetts*.

"Ain't she a beaut?" James said. "Too bad she's not British!"

The other men laughed.

"Doesn't matter what nationality she is—just as long as she gets the job done," Henry said. "All I care is that she's an Allied ship."

James said, "Do we salute? This is an American ship, and they are navy. Paul and I are Royal Air Force."

"Again, let me state that we are an Allied operation," Henry said. "We will salute just like we will all salute the British military when the time comes."

The side of the ship had been painted with odd patterns to throw off the U-boats when aiming their torpedoes. The whole ship was more awesome than Henry had ever seen on films and file photos. Henry took a quick mental inventory on what he saw: massive guns all around, 681 feet stem to stern, and at least two catapults. There were 9 x 16 guns, 20 x 5 guns, 24 x 40 mm cannons, and 35 x 20 mm cannons. That was a total of eighty-eight guns. Somehow, the bombers seemed very much undergunned compared to the mighty war vessel that sat before them now. This mighty ship boasted 681 feet stem to stern and had enough power to push twenty-eight knots. She had a crew compliment of 1,793.

Henry and his team were still admiring the mighty ship's outward appearance when they climbed aboard.

The captain was there to meet them.

"Good evening, gentlemen! I'm Captain Francis E. M. Whiting. It's an honor for us to be included in your operations."

"Good evening, Captain." Henry saluted. "It's a pleasure to be aboard such a massive and powerful ship."

"We'll talk more in the morning," the captain said. "These men will show you to your quarters."

Everyone saluted the captain, and then they were off to find their bunks. The trip to Plymouth, England, would take four days, and it was going to be an interesting trip.

Saint-Nazaire

Adelbert Spangler had received a message on his Enigma machine: "Commandos launched. Four days until arrival. Need cove cleared for drop-off 7/22 at 0200 local time."

The message he sent back confirmed that he understood and that his soldiers would be diverted elsewhere. Spangler moved to the window in his office and folded his arms across his chest. Thoughts raced through his mind about the consequences of his actions. The Nazis were not going to let him live after such a deception, and he would be found out—no two ways about it. Construction would soon be complete, and Spangler knew he would have to make some tough decisions about the Jews who were in the buildings and on the docks.

Spangler made his way down to the construction area to inspect the work.

One of his trusted soldiers, Fritz Adresson, was by his side.

"Construction is almost complete, lieutenant."

"Yes, I know."

"Should we start executing the workers?"

In the past, executions had taken place in the forest where no one could hear the shots. The Nazis had perfected a disposal system for the Jews. The vast majority of the soldiers enjoyed murdering them.

"These Jews won't be executed," said Spangler, hoping that his compassion for these people had not been evident in his voice. "Instead, we'll send them back to the concentration camp that we got them from."

Adresson was confused. The usual plan to exterminate the workers was being changed, and he didn't know why.

"Is there a problem?" inquired Spangler.

"No, sir!" Adresson saluted and walked away.

Spangler was dedicated in his campaign to protect these innocent people. He wondered how he had distanced himself from the Nazi way of thinking and become more compassionate. He made his way back to his office, retrieved his Enigma machine, and sent a coded message.

"Workers are almost done with initial construction."

As he returned the machine to its hiding place, thoughts of death took root. He was indeed a good man, and that didn't fit the mold for the Nazi way of thinking. The thoughts of death didn't bother him; in fact, they were a welcome alternative to being stuck in the Nazi way of life.

Washington, DC

As Jim Mason made his way to the War Room, thoughts of the last message he had gotten from Adelbert Spangler troubled him. How to help the commandos had been in his thoughts before they drew up the plans. How to arm them heavily enough to be effective, and yet lightly enough to not be discovered on the ferry or the bus ride to Saint-Nazaire, was going to be tricky.

Jim entered the War Room deeply troubled. Different members of his military friends spoke to him, yet he was so engrossed in thought that he hadn't noticed them. He placed his briefcase to one side of the table, sat down, and opened the case. He set aside the papers that he would need for his opening statements, and then he set aside the copies for the Joint Chiefs.

The chiefs entered the room and took a seat. The chairman smiled and nodded at Jim, and Jim nodded back. Jim had been before this panel on many occasions, and they had always been kind to him. Most of them were military, and they understood the amount of pressure that the job entailed.

"What's on the agenda for the day?"

"Mr. Jim Mason has some updates," the clerk said.

"Good morning, Mr. Mason. Talk to us," said the chairman.

"Good morning," Jim said. "We've worked most of the night to get together the finishing touches for the Saint-Nazaire commando plans."

"Well, we look forward to hearing them," the chairman said, leaning back in his chair.

"First of all, we've launched the first five members of the team. They are scheduled to arrive in Plymouth, England, on July 22. From there they will pick up a ferry to Roscoff, France, and they will board a bus to Vannes, France. These men will only be armed with M1911 pistols with four clips each. Each clip contains seven bullets."

"If I may interrupt you, Mr. Mason, I have a question," General Hinckley said.

"Of course, General. That's why I'm here."

"Where will the commandos get heavier arms?"

Jim smiled. "That's where it gets interesting, General. If you'll indulge me, I'll get to that very soon." Jim wondered why the general had asked that question, and then he realized that he'd forgotten to give the papers to the panel.

"I do apologize that in the confusion in my mind over this operation, I forgot to give you a copy of the updates."

There was a short rumble of chuckles.

One of the interns came over to Jim, retrieved the papers, and handed them to the chairman.

Jim leafed over to the next page and then continued.

"We're on page 3. The same plan stands for the trip to within eight miles of Saint-Nazaire. No traffic is allowed beyond that point. There aren't any guards there, but travel into the area is a risk—and no bus driver in his right mind would dare go into that area. The Nazis would not hesitate to blow up the bus." Jim looked around the room, and as usual, all eyes were on him. "After departing the bus, the commandos will retrieve their backpacks, which will contain their weapons and ten pounds each of RDX Composition-C."

Jim took a breath and leafed another page.

"They'll have to hike the eight miles to the church, and the plans for evacuation have already been covered. Now here's the kicker."

Jim leafed over a couple of pages and looked up at the Joint Chiefs. They had all scooted up to the edge of their seats and leaned their elbows on the bench.

Jim said, "Lieutenant Spangler, who we all remember is in charge of the dock operations for the Nazis, will clear the armed guard away from the cove. The cove consists of a cave that is dry, at least for the most part, and will be used to store five hundred pounds of RDX Composition-C and an assortment of assault weapons. This cove will be cleared of all Nazi guards tomorrow morning at around 0200. A small supply boat will pull into the shore, and the supplies will be unloaded and camouflaged. Are there any questions?"

There was a flood of questions from the Joint Chiefs, which Jim answered in turn.

After the questions were answered, Jim continued.

"Now comes the tricky part. After the guard has been removed from the area and the supplies have been dropped, Lieutenant Spangler will move the majority of the guards inland. He'll concoct a story of having seen some activity a couple of miles into the forest and up on the next rise above the church. With the docks almost bare of soldiers, the commandos will have more leverage in placing the plastics. They will have a team of divers who will carry ten pounds each of plastics to their designated points of deployment. There is a submarine net located around the dock perimeter, and some of the explosives will be used to take that out along with the structures of the docks. After this is complete, the RDX will be detonated and will cause a chain reaction to all the other placements. After all is done, the commandos will move back up to the rise where the Nazi guards have been sent and will take them out. With the element of surprise, we expect a minimum of casualties."

There was a rustle about the room. Jim looked up at the chairman, and the chairman smiled and nodded at Jim.

Saint-Nazaire

Spangler finished reading his messages on the Enigma machine and realized he would need to talk to the people in the church. He didn't want to, but he knew that in order for his own personal sacrifices to be worth their while, he would have to make them aware of the danger they were in.

He keyed back his responses into the machine and included a message about his plans to approach the church. He would take two armed guards with him, since that was the Nazi way, and instruct the guards to wait to the east of the church. To avoid bringing suspicion on himself, he would explain that the church people would become nervous if they were approached by armed guards.

Spangler was satisfied with this plan of action, but he also wondered how he would be received by the people at the church. Would he have to somehow convince the folks that he was on their side? His intentions were good, but everyone on earth knew that Nazis were ruthless people. He had to convince them that he was not of the Nazi way of thinking.

He would have to wait for nightfall. Not too late though. He didn't want to have to rouse them out of bed. He would have to be unarmed, but he wondered if the people at the church had weapons. Many thoughts occurred to him, but one thing was for certain—he was not planning on surviving for much longer anyway. The operations that were going to take place would soon manifest themselves as being part of his doing, and he was sure to die at the hands of the Nazis.

Spangler's thoughts were abruptly interrupted by a knock on the door. "Enter!"

The door opened and in walked Fritz Adresson.

"You wanted to see me, sir?"

"Yes. I have a job for you."

Fritz seemed nervous about the prospect of being given a task. He was aware that the lieutenant had made some choices in the past that appeared questionable by him and a few other soldiers.

"I'm listening, sir," Fritz replied with a visible uneasiness.

"Settle down, Fritz. This is an easy task."

Fritz sighed and relaxed. "I'm ready to do what you need, sir."

"Good!" Spangler said. "Meet me here at 2100 hours."

"Yes, sir!"

"And I need you to bring another soldier with you. Someone of your own choosing."

Fritz saluted and walked out the door.

Spangler was satisfied that Fritz understood that he needed to bring a soldier with whom he was closely familiar. This operation was going to be touch and go, and Spangler was already uncomfortable with what he had to do. He wanted to save the people of the church from certain death, but he also didn't want to upset the apple cart with the roles everyone else played in the situation. One minor slipup, and he could screw up the whole operation. He certainly had a great deal on his plate! Spangler walked back to the big window in his office and folded his arms across his chest.

Alexandre was sitting at the dinner table with Josephine. He noticed the smile on her face as she stared at her coffee cup, obviously in her own little world. As usual, Alexandre waited for a bit before interrupting her thoughts. "It's good to see you smile."

"Oh. I didn't realize I was smiling."

"Care to share your thoughts?" Alexandre said as he took a sip of his coffee.

"Just thinking about how Emma seems lately. Bill has been the boost she needed. She's in love with him—or did you notice that?"

"I noticed," Alexandre said with a smile.

The smile left Josephine's face, and a frown appeared.

"What's wrong, dear?" inquired a puzzled Alexandre.

"I just hope something doesn't ruin this for them. We were living a happy life before the Nazis ruined that for us. Remember?"

"How could I ever forget that? But nothing could ever ruin the love I have for my family. I hope I've proved that to you over the years."

Josephine looked at her husband and knew that he was right. She also knew that he had something on his mind. The look in his eyes was a dead giveaway—as it always was. "You seem preoccupied, Alexandre."

Alexandre nodded. "I need you to promise me something."

"I'll promise whatever you ask, darling."

Alexandre drew in a breath. "I need you to promise me that you'll leave when it's time to leave."

Josephine had no idea where Alexandre was going with this statement. "What do you mean? Do you know something that I don't?"

"It's inevitable. I had a dream that we were hurried out of here by an unlikely ally. The man was dressed in a Nazi uniform. He had compassion in his eyes, and he was nonthreatening."

There was a moment of silence.

"I don't know what the full meaning of the dream could possibly be," Alexandre said.

"Maybe it was just a dream, dear."

They both knew that his dreams were serious. Alexandre had had dreams before that made it seem that he may be in possession of—at least in a limited form—clairvoyance. Alexandre took Josephine's hand, and they sat in silence.

CHAPTER 13

Henry sat in the galley with the members of his commando crew as they reviewed their plans. It was between mealtimes, so they were all alone. They had their packets laid out on the table and were deep in study. Unfortunately, they could not take the packets with them after they left the ship because they couldn't be caught by the Nazis in possession of such detailed information. They would have to memorize every word.

"Okay. So, let's get down to brass tacks," Henry said.

"Open your packets to page five. This is where we will begin our operations after we land in Plymouth."

An official-looking man walked into the room and saw Henry and his men. He smiled and walked over to their table.

"I hope I'm not interrupting you, gentlemen. My name is Phillip L. Van Landingham Sr. I'm the executive officer of this ship."

The men stood, introduced themselves, and shook Van Landingham's hand.

"You're not interrupting at all, sir!" Henry said. "In fact, we're in your debt for helping us out."

"Not at all. You don't have any debts here. We're deeply honored to be able to help out in this operation."

"So, you're familiar with our plans?" Henry said.

Van Landingham tilted his head to one side and drew in a breath. "I've read the dossier on the operation and each member of your team. I've got to say that I am truly impressed! Eighteen bombing missions unscathed? That's got to be one for the record books!"

"It's all for the cause, sir," Henry said as he bowed his head. "We were just doing our jobs to the best of our abilities."

"That's highly commendable," said Van Landingham as he rose from his chair. "Now if you'll excuse me, I have duties to perform."

The men stood up as he walked away and out into the hallway.

"It looks like we have a great deal of support here," Henry said, "and we will do what we can to earn our keep. Now back to page 5."

Saint-Nazaire, 2100 Hours

Bill and Emma were on the perch. Emma sat in front of Bill on the bench. He had one arm around her waist and the other atop her shoulder with his hand on the binoculars. "Do you have it now?"

"I think so. I'm adjusting the focus."

Bill had been trying to teach Emma a thing or two on spying. They had jokingly given her the title of "Fickle Mistress."

Emma let out a gasp.

"What is it?" asked Bill.

"I see three men walking off the east dock and coming this way."

Bill took the binoculars and had a look for himself. Maybe they were just looking around and wouldn't feel the need to come to the church. Two of the men were obviously soldiers, and the third man was dressed in a Nazi officer's uniform.

The men proceeded toward them, and Bill realized that they were indeed coming to the church.

"They're coming here," Bill said.

Emma was afraid. She remembered what these bad people were capable of doing.

"What are we going to do?"

"We need to get your father," replied Bill.

Bill and Emma scurried out of the perch and went downstairs. Alexandre was nowhere to be seen.

"Father?" Emma called out.

Alexandre came out of the hallway in a trot.

"Yes, dear?"

"You have to see this, sir!" Bill said. He took Alexandre by the arm and led him out into the ruins.

"Look. Over there," Bill said as he handed the binoculars to Alexandre.

Alexandre saw the men coming.

"Go get Mother and tell her to be ready to move," Alexandre said. "And get Rabiah and Father Ambroise out here." Alexandre then looked at Bill and said, "Go check the parachute pack in your closet. Front pouch."

Bill hurried down the stairs and opened the closet. There was a pistol in his parachute pack. He had forgotten that he had packed the weapon before he bailed out of the plane. Bill tucked the pistol into his back pocket and hurried back up to Alexandre.

Emma ran down the stone stairs to deliver the messages.

Very shortly thereafter, there were cries and whines from children being roused. Father Ambroise and Rabiah ran up the stairs and joined Bill and Alexandre. Bill took the binoculars and continued to watch the approaching men. "It looks like they've stopped, and the officer is talking to the soldiers."

The soldiers remained about thirty feet inside of the tree line and the officer continued to proceed forward.

"This is very strange," Bill said as he handed the binoculars back to Alexandre.

"Yes. Very strange indeed," Alexandre said as he gazed.

The officer had made it to the edge of the ruins.

"Good evening," he began. "I'm Lieutenant Adelbert Spangler. I am unarmed. I need to speak to you if that is at all possible."

The four men stood there silently as Spangler doffed his hat to show that there was no weapon on his head. He turned 360 degrees with his hands in the air to show that he was not packing. He then lifted his pant legs to show that he didn't have a weapon strapped to him.

"We're unsure of what to make of this visit, Mr. Spangler," Alexandre said after a short pause.

"Please allow me to approach you. You have my word that this visit is honorable."

"Nazi" and "honorable" didn't seem to fit together, so the men were wary of Spangler's intentions.

"You may approach us," replied a skeptical Alexandre.

Spangler approached the men with his hands in the air. He stopped five feet in front of the group and said, "You are in grave danger. I wish to help you avoid what is coming."

To the men, this admission was confusing. The Nazis had destroyed their homes, and now this officer wanted to help them.

"I see you have doubts, but what I am about to tell you should dispel any fears that you may have. I'm in constant contact with Jim Mason of the OSS and Edward Davies of MI6. May we go inside to talk?"

Alexandre looked at Bill, then looked back at Spangler. Alexandre motioned his hand toward the stairs.

"I suppose you have many questions for me, but first let me introduce you to the problems at hand."

The men looked at each other and wondered what they were going to hear. It wasn't going to be good, they were sure of that.

"Your city was destroyed a little over two years ago on May 18, 1941, by two German ships. The *Bismarck* was one of them, and it has since been sunk. You can take some solace in that."

Spangler continued. "The *Tirpitz* was the other ship. It's still at large, but I'm guessing that its days are numbered as well. One of the commanders on the ship was General Major Josef Kramer. He ordered an overkill, and it sickens me to even have to talk about it."

The men cringed.

Alexandre looked up and saw Emma peeking around the wall of the hallway.

"Would you ask Mother to come make some coffee, dear?" Alexandre said to Emma.

Emma nodded and disappeared around the corner.

Spangler continued, in obvious pain over what he was saying.

"The general major is now in charge of the operations of the dock facilities, and he is talking of destroying the church and killing you."

Spangler had to pause; he needed a break between the pieces of information he was sharing.

Josephine and two of the other ladies had made their way into the dining room where they hesitated. Alexandre motioned to the kitchen, and they slipped past Spangler delicately. Emma followed them into the kitchen.

"How do we avoid the danger?" asked Alexandre.

Spangler had regained his composure and reached into his coat pocket slowly so that he wouldn't be viewed as reaching for a weapon. He retrieved a bundle of papers and handed them to Alexandre.

Alexandre unfolded the papers and began to read. It was a compilation of communications between the OSS and MI6.

"I'm sure you can see by the papers that careful plans have already been made to rescue you. A team of five commandos will arrive in two days. I would suggest that you do as they say."

Josephine, Emma, and one of the other ladies emerged from the kitchen with a tray of coffee cups and a pot of coffee.

Emma took a cup and set it in front of Spangler.

He looked at the ladies and said, "Thank you for the coffee, ladies. I know you hate me, but I assure you that I had nothing to do with the destruction and deaths of your city and your people. I am attempting to make amends for the evil that my people have bestowed on you."

Josephine nodded nervously and retired back into the hallway along with the rest of the ladies.

Emma took a seat next to Bill, and Alexandre nodded in approval of her presence. Emma took Bill by his free hand.

"There is one other issue that I need to discuss with you," continued Spangler. "It is regarding a certain activity that you will notice at or around 0200. There will be a supply boat at the cove unloading weapons and supplies for the commandos and food rations for you good people on your journey to your temporary home, wherever that may be. Don't be alarmed by this. It will be a British ship."

Spangler paused for a moment. "Are there any questions?"

No one had any questions.

Spangler sighed and then said, "Again, let me apologize for the inconvenience that you and your families have been put through due to the indiscretions of my people. I am truly sorry! I guess you've realized by now that I have turned away from my Nazi heritage and am now on the road to making amends."

The men all nodded, still speechless, but thankful that they had an unlikely ally to aid in their survival.

Spangler finished his coffee and stood up. "I'll bid you good night, and if there's anything I can help you with, just send a message. The commandos will have communications to your OSS and MI6, and they can relay messages back to me."

Spangler departed up the stairs and off into the forest.

The men were at a loss for words, so they just sat in silence and drank their coffee. Josephine and the ladies entered the room. Josephine sat next to Alexandre, leaned her head on his chest, and began to weep. Alexandre kissed her on top of the head and pulled her tight.

Washington, DC

Jim entered the office of General Hinckley and walked over to his receptionist's desk.

"Can I help you, Mr. Mason?"

Apparently, he was better known around this place than he realized.

"Can you please ask the general if I can have an audience with him?"

"Of course. Give me a moment, please."

The receptionist picked up her phone, and Jim stepped back a little to examine his paperwork.

"The general will see you, Mr. Mason."

Jim entered the office, and the general smiled and stood up.

"Good to see you, Mr. Mason. I don't believe we've ever had the pleasure of speaking in person."

"You can call me Jim, sir. Everyone else does, so you shouldn't have to be the exception to the rule."

Norman Hinckley was a five-star general and was a member of the Joint Chiefs of Staff. He deserved all the recognition and respect that could possibly be afforded. "I'm guessing this is not a social call, Jim?"

"I wish it were, sir. I'd be able to sleep some nights if I could socialize."

The general chuckled. "So, what can I do for you?"

Jim placed a packet of papers on the general's desk and began to speak. "These are current radar placements for all ships within 1,500 kilometers of the British coast. Our commandos are on a ship that has just entered this area."

"It looks like they're headed into a little trouble," the general said.

"A 'little trouble' is stating it mildly, sir. I'm here to ask for a safety net—or some extra help in this area."

"Hang tight for a second. I'll make a call."

Jim sat back in his seat as the general picked up his phone.

The general finished his phone call, and Jim could tell by the look on his face that it was good news.

"We've got a few ships just north of the heavy traffic, so they'll be diverted down that way. We've also got promised support from the British."

"That's good news, General. I just hope all of this works."

The general studied Jim's face for a few moments and then said, "You worry too much."

"Excuse me, sir?"

"I said that you worry too much. Do you think my job is easy?"

Jim thought for a moment.

"No, sir. I know it's probably one of the toughest jobs at the Pentagon."

"Do you know why this job is tough?"

"Probably because you have many lives in your hands?"

"That's absolutely right. Do you have any idea how many lives have been lost because I had no choice but to make certain decisions?"

"No, sir," Jim said, feeling uncomfortable.

"So many that I've lost count. But you can't think about lives lost. Decisions are made, and the higher-ups agree on those decisions. If certain decisions kill a certain amount of people, then not making decisions will kill more in the long run."

Jim relaxed a little.

"All of the plans that you've made have been approved by heads that are higher up than either one of us. If deaths occur, then sure, you'll lose sleep. Probably lots of sleep. But just be assured that you made the right decisions."

"Thank you, General. I needed to hear that," Jim said.

CHAPTER 14

"We're receiving a distress signal, sir. The *Aaron Ward* destroyer class is under attack from a German battleship."

"Plot course to intercept," said Captain Whiting. "Range to target?"

"Twelve thousand meters, sir."

The captain was aware of the range of the guns, and he also knew that firing on an enemy with a friendly nearby was risky. "Sound the alarms. All hands to battle stations!"

"Eleven thousand meters and closing, sir. Three minutes to range."

"Status of the executive officer?"

"The XO is already en route, sir: 10,800 meters and closing. We're registering aircraft inbound from the south."

— ◆ —

Henry and his men heard the alarms and were already scrambling out to find something they could do to help.

"Let's head to the guns and see if we can find a place to be of use," Henry said.

Executive Officer Phil Van Landingham had made it to the bridge. "Have we got an update?"

"Ten thousand meters and closing, sir. The ship that's firing on the *Aaron Ward* is the *Tirpitz*."

"Ah!" muttered the captain. "So we finally meet!"

The captain had heard stories of the death and mayhem that had been caused by this ship. The drive and the determination to sink the *Tirpitz* had already boiled to the surface.

"Nine thousand, two hundred meters to target and closing, sir."

"What do you think, Phil?" the captain said.

"We're in range, sir. I say we fire," replied the XO.

"Lock all main guns on the *Tirpitz* and fire when ready," the captain barked.

There was a shudder throughout the ship as the mighty guns fired.

"All guns fired, sir. Range to target is four seconds."

"Let's just hope we don't hit the *Aaron Ward*," the captain muttered.

"Sir, 82 percent direct hits."

"What's the status on the *Aaron Ward*?"

"She's heavily damaged, sir. They have started abandoning ship and are requesting rescue support."

The inbound fighter planes had already started firing on the *Massachusetts*. There was heavy gunfire to the midsection.

"Maintain heading and speed until we get to fifteen hundred meters. I want to crawl between them and the *Tirpitz* to protect them."

"Six thousand meters and closing, sir. Too many enemy fighters to count."

"I need you to supervise the gunners," said the captain to the XO.

"Yes, sir!" said Van Landingham as he went through the door. He ran down the internal gangplanks and happened to meet up with Henry and his men.

"We're here to help," panted Henry.

"Good. We may need it," replied Van Landingham.

They reached the midship turrets, and they scrambled to assist.

"Fifteen hundred meters, sir!"

"Engines to one-quarter. Engage all forward guns and fire."

The ship shuddered again as the guns fired. The *Tirpitz* returned fire, but it was a weak response since it had already been damaged by the *Aaron Ward* and the initial volley from the *Massachusetts*.

The *Massachusetts* shuddered slightly as it was hit by shells.

"Damage report?"

"None available yet, sir. I'll try to get an update."

The shells that were hurled at the *Tirpitz* were a huge success—the ship was burning in a large inferno. But the worries were not over. Dozens of fighter planes had swooped in, and it appeared as if the fight was just beginning.

"Pull alongside the *Aaron Ward*. Let's start evacuation," the captain said.

"Damage reports coming in, sir. Minor damage to midsections. No casualties reported as of yet."

The planes had already started firing at the *Massachusetts*. The turret gunners were hard at work, and multiple hits were recorded. Lots of birds were smoking and burning.

"We've got American and British fighters on the radar, sir," the navigational officer said.

"Thank God!" the captain said.

Heavy fire from the turrets had disabled many of the FW-190 fighters, causing them to plunge into the sea. The *Massachusetts* was being pelted as fighters swooped over and dumped a hail of bullets and then rotated around to more passes.

"Incoming!" one of the turret gunners screamed.

Van Landingham looked up and saw a ball of fire coming right at the turret position. They had set a plane on fire—and it was making a beeline for the midsection of the ship. The plane collided with the turret position and collapsed the shielding for the gunner. Two of the turret gunners were killed instantly.

Henry grabbed one of the positions, and Van Landingham grabbed the other. They were fighting with no shielding, and it was going to be an uphill battle to survive.

"Damage to the midsection, Captain. Two turret gunners are down. Shielding has been breached!"

"We'll have to fight it out with the turrets that are available. We can't risk friendly fire with antiaircraft shells." The captain shook his head. "May God have mercy on us!"

Henry and the XO continued to shoot in what seemed to be one long firing session. Many FW-190s were crashing into the sea as the Allied fighters reached position and had begun to mop up the already-shattered Nazi forces. There were no more incoming planes. Van Landingham and Henry stepped back from the guns.

"Nice shooting, sir!" Henry said.

Van Landingham didn't respond and instead pulled open the right side of his coat. There was a large bloodstain on his shirt. He staggered back against the wall and slid down to a seated position.

"The XO is down!" Henry screamed.

There was an echo of feet scrambling down the gangplank.

"It's okay," said Van Landingham, struggling to speak.

"It's never okay," Henry said.

"No. It's okay. We crushed the enemy forces here with minimal damages and minimal loss of life." The XO smiled as he tripped over his words.

"It's going to be okay," Henry said, trying to be soothing even though he knew that it wasn't going to be.

"Please find my wife and tell her that I love her," Van Landingham said as he went limp. He smiled in death, and the smile never left his face.

Henry pulled the XO close and just sat there holding him.

The medics arrived, and one of them said, "You'll have to let go of him, sir."

Henry looked up at the medic and nodded.

The medics took Van Landingham away.

Henry sat against the wall, looking out through the hole in the turret shielding. He had witnessed true heroism. *Heroes were dead. Right?* He realized a new definition for the word *hero* that day. Henry also realized that he, himself, was not a hero. He was just another body to fill a hole. Van Landingham, the XO, was a hero, and it was going to be Henry's mission to make sure that he was honored to the degree that heroes should be honored. Even after being struck by the bullet, the XO had held his ground. Henry wondered if he would ever be able to do the same.

Saint-Nazaire, July 20, 1943, 0130

It was going to be a sleepless night. Bill sat at the table with Alexandre, Rabiah, and Father Ambroise. Emma was by Bill's side, and he was holding her hand.

"Anyone have any thoughts?" Alexandre said, finally breaking the silence.

"Well," began Bill, "we have to make a contingency plan just in case the commandos aren't able to make it to us."

All the men looked at Bill, and he suddenly felt that he was being chosen the leader of the idea circle. The reality was that none of the men were equipped with any idea of how they were going to slip past all the soldiers. Their families' lives were at stake as well.

"We need to bat around a few ideas, no matter how weak they sound, and then formulate a plan around those ideas," Bill said. "The cold hard fact is that we won't be able to slip out of here without help."

Alexandre shrugged and said, "We've been told by Lieutenant Spangler that General Major Kramer is going to kill us when he gets back from his trip. We need to get a plan together in case the commandos don't get here in time, as much as I hate to overstate the obvious."

"We all agree on that," Rabiah said. "I suggest that we start packing in the morning. What can we take that won't slow us down or make us a target?"

"That's a good start," Father Ambroise said. "We need to figure out what we need to survive. Our people are good hunters, so we can feed ourselves once we get situated somewhere."

Bill looked at Emma, and she was shaking her head.

Bill tightened his grip on Emma's hand and cleared his throat. "I need to get back up to the bomber."

All eyes were on Bill, but no one spoke. Emma looked at the floor and loosened her grip on Bill's hand.

"I know you don't like this, Emma, but I've got to make sure the waist gun is working."

Emma looked at Bill and tightened her grip on his hand. "Then I'm going with you."

The men in the room looked at Emma.

Alexandre said, "As much as it pains me to say this, I'm going to agree with you, dear. I trust you, and I know you've grown a great deal." Alexandre looked away and hoped that he'd made the right decision. The other men looked at Alexandre like he'd lost his mind. Alexandre ignored the glares.

"Please excuse me."

Rabiah and Father Ambroise stood up and bid their good nights and went to be with their families.

Bill and Emma made their way to the perch, and they watched as the ship unloaded the supplies in the cove.

Bill pulled her close and kissed her lips.

Emma laid her head on his chest, and, surprisingly, they both fell fast asleep.

Plymouth, England, July 22, 1943, 0215

The USS *Massachusetts* arrived at the port at Plymouth, and Henry and the team readied themselves to depart the ship. As they made their way off the gangplank, they saw the caskets of the three men who had died in the action just two hours before. The captain stood beside the caskets.

"Thank you for helping us, sir," Henry said.

"Thank you for your help in repelling the enemy," the captain said.

There was silence for a moment as the five men saluted the dead.

"I have something for you, Lieutenant." The captain handed Henry a picture of Executive Officer Van Landingham. "This picture is actually a year old. We took it while we were in port to receive this ship. It's a picture of happier times."

"I'll keep this picture, Captain. It's a picture of a true war hero, and I'll display it proudly whenever I find myself in combat."

"Go kick some butt!" the captain said as he saluted.

Henry saluted the captain, and he and his team headed for the ferry. Henry took the picture, wrapped it in a cloth, and put it in a pocket of his backpack.

Morning had come, and the sun was just about to rise on Saint-Nazaire. Bill woke, and Emma was against his chest. She was obviously still asleep. He sat in silence for a few minutes before he woke her. "Wake up, dear. The sun is rising."

Emma rubbed her eyes. The sunrise was lovelier than she'd ever seen. She was with the man she loved, and everything was more beautiful when she was with him. She stood up and moved over between Bill's knees. She leaned back against him and rested her head against his shoulder.

"The only thing more beautiful than this sunrise is you, baby," Bill whispered in her ear.

Emma smiled. She had never been in love before.

"I have something to ask you," Bill whispered as he kissed her ear.

"Ask me anything."

"I hate to break up this embrace, but I need to go get something." Emma was bewildered, but she stood up and Bill ran down the stairs to the church. Emma was very confused, and yet she was also very interested to know what Bill had to retrieve.

Two minutes later, Bill ran back up the stairs. He had his right hand clenched like he was holding something. Bill knelt before Emma and took her left hand.

"I love you more than life itself. I've loved you since the first day I laid eyes on you."

Emma's breath quickened, and she began to shiver.

"Will you marry me?"

Tears welled up in Emma's eyes as she bobbed her head up and down. "Yes! Yes, you silly man. I'll marry you!"

Bill leaned forward, kissed her lips, and put the ring on her finger.

Emma grabbed Bill, held him close, and wept tears of joy.

"This ring is not perfect, and it's made of copper, but it's the only thing I had to give you. I made this ring when I was ten. We'll get you a suitable ring when the time comes."

"I don't care what it looks like. I love it!" Emma said.

"I will have to ask your father for his blessing, but I'm sure that won't be a problem."

"Even if he says no, I'll run away with you," Emma said.

"I'm going to make a suggestion," Bill said. "I'd like to get married as soon as possible. We're about to have trouble here, and I want you to be my wife before we have to move. Is that okay with you?"

"It's perfect! Let's go talk to Father and Father Ambroise!"

Roscoff, France, July 22, 1943, 0800

The commandos completed the ferry ride and arrived in Roscoff, France. They had entered enemy-occupied territory and were pretty much on their own. They had cleared the Nazi guard at the ferry dock with amazing ease as the papers they had been given were very concise. They had been given vichy for money to make them blend in. Everything about them was authentic, from identification to the clothing they wore.

Now came the time for the bus ride. They were on schedule to make it to Saint-Nazaire at around 1800 local time.

Saint-Nazaire, July 22, 1943, 0815

Bill and Emma entered the dining area holding hands. Emma was smiling, and Bill was nervous.

"Good morning," Alexandre said with a smile.

Rabiah and Father Ambroise smiled and lifted their coffee cups as if giving a toast of sorts.

Bill and Emma sat down, with Bill next to Alexandre and Emma to the left of Bill. All nervousness had left Emma in light of her joy. Alexandre wrinkled his face as he sensed that he was about to be drawn into conversation.

"You two have something on your minds?"

"Yes, sir," Bill said. "We need to speak with you."

"We can leave you alone," said Rabiah as he looked at Father Ambroise.

"No. It's okay. We don't mind that you hear this."

Alexandre folded his arms across his chest and waited for Bill to speak.

Bill seemed to be in thought, shaking his head and moving his lips. Was he rehearsing what he was going to say? Bill lifted Emma's hand to his lips and kissed the back of it lightly.

"Well, sir, I need to ask for your daughter's hand in marriage."

"And you've both discussed this?"

"Yes, sir."

"And, Emma, do you love this man?"

"I do, Father. I will always love Bill," Emma said, choking back tears of pure joy.

Alexandre sat back. He didn't actually have a problem with them getting married, but he figured he'd let them squirm for a bit. Alexandre shot a glance over at Rabiah and Father Ambroise, and they were both smiling. He then looked back over at Bill and Emma. They looked nervous.

Alexandre leaned forward and said, "You have my blessing, young man."

Emma squeaked like a church mouse. Bill breathed a long sigh of pure relief.

"Go get your mother, dear. She needs to be in on this."

Emma left the room like a bullet, shrieking all the way down the long hall.

The men looked at one another in amazement that one person could be so happy over anything given the circumstances that they were in.

Emma returned, dragging Josephine with her.

"What is it, dear?" asked her bewildered mother.

"We're getting married!"

Josephine smiled and hugged Emma. She walked around the table and hugged Bill, and Emma joined in the hug.

Alexandre stood up and decided to join in the group hug as well.

After all was said and done, the four of them sat down again, with Bill holding Emma's right hand and Josephine holding her left.

Bill looked at Alexandre and said, "Emma and I are going to the bomber tonight, and we'd like to be married before we go."

Josephine nodded.

Bill looked at Father Ambroise and said, "We'd like for you to officiate the ceremony."

"I'd be honored to do so," Father Ambroise said.

"Then it's settled." Alexandre got off his chair and shook Bill's hand. He kissed Emma on the forehead, and then he kissed Josephine. Alexandre returned to his seat and took another sip of his coffee. "Welcome to the family, son."

It had come time to pack up what few belongings the families could carry on their exodus from the church home. No one wanted to have to leave the area since it was where most of them had been born and raised.

Bill and Emma were sitting on the bed in the front bedroom. It was the same room where Bill had spent nearly two months recuperating. There was a knock at the door.

Bill looked up and said, "Come, come."

Emma giggled. Bill looked at Emma and just shrugged in a cartoonish way. The door opened, and Alexandre said, "Can I bother you for a few minutes?"

"Sure. You're not a bother, sir."

"It looks like you've got a few things packed. You're making good progress here."

"Thank you, sir," Bill said. "We don't have much to pack."

Alexandre's face became serious. Bill looked at Emma, and she looked just as bewildered as Bill.

"What I needed to talk to you about was the pistol that I knew was in your parachute pack."

"Yes, sir. I was wondering about that myself."

"I found that pistol when we pulled you off the beach on the day of the bombing. The pocket that the gun was in was torn open, and it was lying on the ground. I picked it up and put it back in the pack, in a different pocket—one that was not so torn."

"I packed that pistol as I was bailing out of the plane. It was sliding across the floor. I knew I may need to protect myself if and when I made it to the ground," Bill said.

"Anyway, Father Ambroise would like to see you two when you get a chance."

"We'll go see him right away, sir."

"And stop calling me *sir*. You're about to be my son," Alexandre said. He patted Bill on the shoulder and smiled.

Emma grinned.

Saint-Malo-de-Guersac, France, July 22, 1943, 1500

The bus ride had ended, and from this point forward, the trip would have to be completed on foot.

Henry and his crew grabbed their backpacks and slipped into the forest.

"We'll have to stay in the forest and slip into Saint-Nazaire just north of the church," Henry said. "We just need to keep a pace that's quick but not too quick. We've got to be on the lookout for booby traps," Henry said as he looked at his watch. "I estimate our time of arrival to be around 1745 local time. I just hope that somehow these people know we're coming. We may not be received too well if not."

These men were trained commandos, and they knew all too well what lay in front of them.

Washington, DC, the Pentagon

The phone rang.

"Jim Mason."

"Hey, Jim. It's Ed."

"Hey, Ed. How goes the world over there?"

"Just thought I'd let you know that the commando crew you sent made it to England around 0145 this morning."

"Well, that's a good thing! I'm glad to hear it!"

"Just one other thing I forgot to tell you, Jim."

"And what's that?"

"We left a little gift in the stash at the cove. It's an Enigma machine. You'll probably hear from them as soon as they slip it out of the cove. Hopefully, Spangler will have the troops situated where they won't have to fight their way in."

"Let's hope not, Ed."

"I'm still looking forward to seeing you."

"I'll try to get over there soon, Ed. Take care."

Jim hung up the phone and reflected on the amount of stress that this operation had caused him over the past few weeks. Even after the conversation with the general, he would still hold himself accountable for the deaths that would undoubtedly happen.

Jim stood up, walked over to the window, and looked out. It was a nice sunny day, and all was peaceful. He could only imagine the death and mayhem that was occurring on battlefields and in the sky across the ocean. He just shook his head and wondered.

Saint-Nazaire, July 22, 1943, 1545

Bill and Emma stepped out of the bedroom and into the dining room, where they saw the usual three men sitting around drinking coffee.

"Come and join us," said Father Ambroise with a smile on his face. "It's good to see the lovebirds!"

The two sat down by Alexandre and opposite Rabiah and Father Ambroise.

"We've come to talk to you, Father Ambroise," Bill said.

"Good. Then we'll skip the formalities. I think we know each other well enough to skip the questions about love. I know you love her—and she loves you. I've seen you together enough to know that you do, in fact, love each other."

"Yes!" Bill said.

"Of course!" Emma smiled.

"Good. Then we'll draw up a contract of sorts that we'll all sign, and you'll be married. All we'll have to do is the ceremony."

CHAPTER 15

Spangler stood on the dock as the transport boat arrived, bringing his tormentor back to Saint-Nazaire. General Major Josef Kramer had returned, and Spangler was not looking forward to having to deal with him. The return of Kramer meant less freedom for Spangler to help anyone do much of anything.

The boat docked. Kramer stepped off and immediately growled. "Oh. It's you."

"It's good to see you too, sir," said Spangler.

"You're such a rotten liar." Kramer shook his head.

"I trust you had a pleasant trip, sir?"

"It was business, not a vacation. I was looking forward to getting back here to finish a few pet projects," said Kramer as he raised his binoculars. "I see the church is still standing. There isn't much activity from the vermin."

Kramer continued to scan the scene at the church.

"Do you know what I got to do on this trip, Spangler?"

"I'm sure it's none of my business, sir."

"Of course it's none of your business. I just want to brag." Kramer shot Spangler a sideways glance.

"It's your privilege to brag, sir. I'm all ears." Spangler didn't want to hear about the deviousness that the general major had bestowed on anyone, but he was trapped into listening. He already knew what this excuse for a human being was capable of.

"I had the rare pleasure of torturing the Jew vermin myself," said Kramer with a devilish grin.

Spangler became immediately nauseated. He honestly thought he was going to vomit right there on the dock.

"We rid the world of fifteen thousand in the few days that I was gone. And now we're about to rid the world of a bunch of church vermin."

Spangler was aghast at this revelation—even though he was accustomed to the demon talk of Kramer. Spangler had done all he could do. Now that the general major was back, he couldn't do anything to further warn the poor souls in the church. He could only hope that the commandos would arrive in time.

"We'll wait for nightfall—and carry out our riddance!"

July 22, 1943, 1745

The wedding party had gathered. All twenty-six people in the church home had come together. It had been a long day of packing up belongings, and they were ready for a break. This joyous time was just what they needed. After all the misery of losing their city, and their friends, this wedding was going to be one last celebration before moving on to a new life.

Father Ambroise and Bill walked into the large dining room. Everyone else, except for Emma and her mother, was seated at the table. Alexandre got up from his seat and joined them in the far corner of the dining room by the kitchen door. They didn't have any musical instruments, so one of the ladies would sing a hymn as Emma entered the room. Alexandre had dual jobs: he would give Emma away and be Bill's best man.

Emma and her mother entered the room. Alexandre linked his arm into Emma's, and they slowly walked up the long aisleway to Bill and Father Ambroise. Emma was beautiful. She was dressed all in white, and even though it wasn't a wedding dress, it still made her look radiant. Emma was carrying a small bundle of wildflowers that she had picked earlier in the afternoon.

Emma and her father had finished the walk, and Alexandre took his place next to Bill.

No one had noticed that Henry had stepped down the stairs and was standing by the end of the stairway. The other four commandos were crouched outside and watching the dock.

"And who is here to give this woman away?" Father Ambroise asked.

"Well, I'd give her away, but this guy's a bum," Henry said as he smiled.

Everyone in the church was startled.

Bill wheeled around while putting his hand on his pistol. He had made it a habit to carry it in his pocket. "Henry?"

"Well, you guessed that one right, old buddy. Glad to see you remember your old pal."

Bill walked quickly to Henry. He didn't know what to think. Was this part of his nightmare? Of course it wasn't. Henry was an old friend and certainly not a nightmare! Bill threw his arms around Henry, and they hugged and slapped each other on the back.

"You're listed as KIA, old friend. You might want to set them straight. Can't have dead men getting married."

"If you don't mind me asking, are you a commando now?"

"Yup. Got kicked up to lieutenant here a couple weeks ago."

Bill looked at Alexandre, who stepped aside.

"Your friend is our friend. He needs to be your best man."

"I saw you half draw that pistol out of your pants, bud. If your wife-to-be doesn't mind a couple of pistol packers standing next to her, I'd be delighted to be your best man."

Emma smiled. She was a little confused as to who Henry was, but she was willing to get to know him. He was Bill's friend, and she was going to want to make friends with him as well. She nodded her approval.

Bill and Henry took their places next to her. The ceremony continued, and the people in the church were tearful.

Alexandre also got misty-eyed but claimed there was dust in the air.

When the wedding was over, Bill knew that they had to get down to the business of evacuation. Henry looked at Bill and gave him a knowing nod.

"I have to go talk to Henry."

"I'm going with you."

"It's business, dear."

"I don't care. I'm going with you."

Bill took Emma by the hand and went up top to talk to Henry.

It was just dusk, and they had to hurry to get the church evacuated.

"Me and the team have to get down to the cove to get some heavier armament. All we have are pistols."

Henry introduced his team to Bill and Emma.

"I'll go with you," Bill said.

"No, buddy. You just got married. Can't risk getting you hurt."

"I'll keep watch then. I've got my pistol and a pair of binoculars."

"We'll be back as quick as we can." Henry motioned for the others to get moving.

Bill and Emma moved up to the perch and watched the dock and the progress of the commando team.

"We should have gotten married sooner," Emma said.

Bill was silent for a moment.

"What's wrong, Bill?" Emma asked, sensing a problem.

Bill sighed. He wasn't looking forward to what he had to say.

"I need you to go with your family. I have to stay—at least for a little while."

"If you have to stay, then I'm staying with you."

Bill knew this was going to be an uphill battle.

"You can't stay, dear. I would never forgive myself if something happened to you."

"What about you? We just got married, and now I have to lose you on our wedding night?"

"I'm a soldier. I can't leave my buddies behind. I love you, Emma, but I've got to insist that it be this way. I'll catch up with you as soon as I can. I promise!"

Emma was fighting a losing battle against her tears.

"I want to protect you, darling. I need you to go find your father and stay by his side. I'll come get you when it's time."

"I want to stay here with you."

"I need you to do as I ask. I want to protect you. I love you. Now go. Please."

Emma wept as she went down the stairs into the church.

Bill felt badly about the circumstances, but he didn't have much of a choice.

The team had returned with five sacks.

"We've got five Bren light machine guns and a mess of ammo," Henry said. "And we've got a couple of bags of food for the church members."

"Good. We're going to need some firepower," Bill said.

"We? Oh no, buddy. You just got married."

"Well, I'm a soldier, and I'm not leaving you guys to fend for yourselves without me helping you."

James Bartow said, "We've got company! Five soldiers approaching!"

Henry grabbed his binoculars. They were about two hundred yards and closing. They didn't seem to be in a big hurry. "They obviously don't know we're here."

The soldiers made their way out of the tree line. There were four soldiers and one officer. It was time for the commandos to stand their ground and protect the people in the church. Bill and the commandos had taken cover and hoped they had not been seen.

The soldiers had reached the area in front of the ruins.

"Hello, young lady," snarled Kramer. "We're here to put you out of your misery."

Bill looked behind him, and there stood Emma at the top of the stairs. Henry shook his head at Bill, but Bill instinctively stood up and began firing.

The Nazi soldiers had not seen this coming.

The other commandos began firing from behind their hiding places while trying to conceal themselves. If the Nazis knew there were others there besides Bill, then it could create a problem.

Four of the Nazi soldiers lay dead. Kramer was the only one left standing. He had his Luger drawn and pointed at Bill.

Bill had run out of bullets, but he still wanted to maintain the bluff.

"Bill!" screamed Emma.

Kramer laughed and then paused.

"So, your name is Bill. The only reason that I don't kill you here, Bill, is because I know you're being covered. Are those church people that were helping you kill my men—or are those soldiers as well? I'm guessing you're an American soldier. Here's what's going to happen … Bill. I'm going to walk away. If you choose to shoot me, then so be it. I'm not afraid of death." Kramer paused and then scowled as he spoke.

"Nazis are strong people. You Americans and your Allies are weak and pathetic! You'll be crushed like the weaklings that you are! This won't be the last time that we meet … Bill!"

Kramer put his Luger back into its holster, snarled, and then turned around and walked away.

Bill just stood there with the empty pistol in his hand.

Alexandre had come up the stairs and had taken Emma by the arm and led her back down the stairs very quickly. Bill, Henry, and the team followed them down the stairs.

Emma was sobbing.

"I'm so sorry!"

"Honey, it's okay," Bill said.

Henry said, "We have to get you good people out of here. Is there another way out?"

"We've got a cellar door that leads out of the back of the church," Alexandre said.

"We need to get there now! These Nazis are probably mounting a counter attack as we speak," barked Henry.

The families took their simple bags of clothing and made their way out of the cellar to the back of the church. They were concealed from the view of the dock as they made their way into the forest.

"We'll get these folks to Saint-Malo-de-Guersac. We saw an abandoned warehouse that we can use to safely hide them."

Emma hung back with Bill.

"We knew this was going to happen. I love you. I'll come get you when I can. I promise that to you."

Bill hugged Emma tightly. Emma didn't fight him on his decision. She knew that he was doing the right thing. She knew that he would protect her and the church family.

"I love you!" Emma said as Alexandre came to get her.

"Be safe, my son," Alexandre said as he winked.

Bill nodded. "Take care of my wife and our family."

The church family exited quietly into the forest with four of the commandos watching over them.

"We need to get out of here before the soldiers find us," Henry said.

"I know the perfect place," Bill smiled as he spoke.

"I do like perfect places," Henry said with a smirk.

Bill and Henry dragged the last two bags up the hill to the bomber.

"Just looks like a matted bunch of trees," Henry said.

"You're about to be surprised!"

The two men made their way through the trees, and Henry recognized what was in front of him.

"Is this the plane you were on?"

"Yes. It's a miracle that it crashed so close, and it's not that badly damaged."

"Wow!" Henry said. "The fuselage is in relatively good shape."

"Get ready for the best part."

"I'm already giddy. Show me! Show me!"

They stepped through the hole in the fuselage and shined their flashlights on the six, thousand-pound high-explosive bombs still in the rack.

Henry staggered back as he sucked in a deep breath. "Wow! This will be a tremendous asset when the time comes! We can booby-trap this thing with plastics. That will take out a square mile!"

"That's not all, buddy," Bill said. "Follow me."

Bill and Henry headed to the back of the plane. There were the waist guns.

Bill said, "The gun on the left is pretty much damaged beyond repair, but the one on the right will probably function with a little work."

"Any of the other guns working in here?"

"No. We were hit with 88-millimeter shells, and they took out the rear and upper turrets. Another shell took out the lower turret and set the bomb bay on fire. I'm sorry to say that we lost the men too."

Upon hearing of the loss of life, Henry took off his hat as a show of respect for the downed airmen.

"So what we have here is three tons of high-explosive bombs and a supposedly working waist gun."

"It's better than nothing," remarked Henry said as he put his hat back on.

Henry reached into his coat pocket and took out the picture of Van Landingham.

"And speaking of heroes, here's a real hero," Henry said as he handed the picture to Bill.

Bill looked at the picture, and it sparked a sense of recognition in him.

"I had a dream some time ago, and I seem to remember something that reminded me of this man."

Henry took the picture and put it back in his pocket.

"It's a good sign then. You just may have a guardian angel."

Henry opened the bags to look and see what they had recovered as far as weaponry was concerned. Lots of ammo, grenades, a spool of twine, and a machine that neither of the men had ever seen before. It had a book attached to it with a note: "This is an Enigma machine for sending and receiving messages. Read the manual to understand how it works."

Bill took out his binoculars and looked back down the long hill to the church. He could see flashlights as they lit up an area around the church. He really hoped and prayed that the families were safe.

The families were making good time with the coaxing of the commando team. The smaller children were being carried by the adults, and most of them were fast asleep.

Mark Banion and James Bartow had light machine guns and grenades—in case they had to fight. They moved ahead to scout for mines and booby traps.

The plan was for the four commandos to stay with the families and for Bill and Henry to stay in the target area to prepare for the upcoming mission. Everyone knew their jobs, and everyone was determined to make sure the mission worked perfectly.

Once the families arrived in Saint-Malo-de-Guersac, there would be a canvass of the area to find natives of the city who were willing to take in the refugees. It was going to be an uphill battle, but it would have to be done. In the meantime, there was an abandoned warehouse that the team had seen when they got off the bus. It wasn't ideal, but it would do in a pinch.

After the Nazi soldiers had cleared the church for entry, Kramer entered and had a look around. He had brought Spangler with him.

"Vermin!" growled Kramer. "When I find the one called 'Bill,' I'll kill him myself!"

Kramer gritted his teeth and spewed a few swear words.

Spangler just stood quietly by,

"And you!" said Kramer. "You are worthless! You sent the Jews back to the concentration camps instead of exterminating them?"

Actually, Spangler had sent them out on a ship, but had alerted the Allies, and the Allies captured the ship. The Jews had been taken to Bermuda where they would be cared for and nursed back to health. They would then be released, both to America and England. It had been a joint effort thanks to Jim Mason and Director Edward Davies.

"Should we go after them, sir?" Spangler asked.

"No! Let them crawl away like the bottom-feeders they are! When we take over this godforsaken country, they'll be executed! We'll be free from the sewer vermin for good!"

Spangler was truly sickened. Before his eventual death, he knew that he would have to have a hand in destroying Kramer—it was just a matter of careful planning and time. He would certainly need the help of Jim Mason. That was for sure!

Bill peered through his binoculars. "It looks like the soldiers are retreating back to the docks."

Henry heaved a sigh of relief. If push had come to shove, he knew that he and Bill would have had to have done everything in their power to stop them. He was glad that the soldiers had not gone into the woods to find the families.

"I'd say it's a Christmas miracle, but it ain't Christmas."

"You probably need to grab some sleep, brother."

"My team hasn't slept in thirty-six hours. I can't sleep knowing what they have to do before sleeping." Bill continued to watch the soldiers as they filed onto the east dock and back to the main docks.

"Care to fill me in on the details of the mission?"

Henry paused for a moment to get his thoughts in gear. It was going to be a difficult struggle to get all the plans meshed together now that Kramer was back, and they wouldn't be able to get much help from Spangler.

"There are forty-five more commandos on the way. They are supposed to be split up a day apart for departure."

"Will that be enough?"

"We'll have to make do," Henry said. "But first, I have to get this contraption figured out."

Henry grabbed the Enigma machine and turned it in all directions to get an idea of what it was.

"When all else fails, read the instructions," Bill said in a sarcastic voice.

Henry looked at Bill and wrinkled his face in retaliation for the sarcasm. He then took out the instructions and waved them at Bill to show that he was going to read them.

"I'm going to read them. Okay, smart guy?"

Bill laughed and then returned to his watch of the area through his binoculars. Bill put his hand up at Henry.

Henry became quiet and didn't move a muscle. He could hear voices that seemed a short distance away.

A group of three Nazi soldiers had emerged from the tree line, and they were smoking cigarettes. The soldiers were laughing and joking in German, and neither Bill nor Henry could understand the language.

After a few minutes, the group moved back toward the docks.

Bill looked at Henry.

"I guess the plane is hidden well enough to where no one pays a bit of attention to it."

"That's another blessing to add to our list, my friend!" Henry said.

Henry continued to read the instructions.

This thing would be difficult to figure out, but they would get it done. The first page of the instructions contained a handwritten letter from Edward Davies and read as follows:

To use the machine, first turn it on. The power button is on the left side at the back. You'll hear it hum to life. Next, dial the code 5476ght67hy into the dials. This will channel all messages directly to a catch service that will forward the messages to me. The messages will be heavily encrypted and will not change until the operation is complete.

Your friend,
Edward P. Davies.

"I guess we could give this thing a try," Henry said.

Henry turned on the power switch, and the Enigma hummed to life. He dialed in the code sequence and began to type a message:

Families are safe. William C. McLaughton of the US Air Force has been found alive and well and will assist us with operation. Awaiting further instructions.

Lieutenant Henry Jenkins

Henry hit the send button and then sat back. He wasn't sure how the message was being sent or how it would be received. All that mattered was that he had followed the instructions that he was given.

The march had continued to progress at a steady pace, and they had completed three and a half miles. Only four miles to go! The families were tired, but they knew they had to keep going. Sheer will and determination played a big role.

Emma looked straight forward with a blank expression and held her mother's hand.

Alexandre looked at his watch. Nine o'clock. He had volunteered to hold two children during the march, and they were sound asleep. As he had checked his watch, he had had to move his arm up a bit. The movement roused the little girl he was holding on his left shoulder. She looked at him, smiled, and then went back to sleep.

Washington, DC, 1600 Local Time

Jim sat at his desk in an almost comatose state. His mind had ventured so far into the safety of the people in the church that he couldn't think of anything else. He didn't even know the people, but even so, he was deeply concerned for their safety. Jim had read the message that was sent by Henry and was now trying to think of something that could help in even a miniscule way. He found himself wishing that the operation was finished so he could finally get some rest.

Jim was snapped out of his trance when he noticed that the phone was ringing.

"Jim Mason."

"Hey, Jim. It's Ed."

"Hey, Ed. How are things across the pond?" Jim said rather glumly.

"You sound down and out, Jim. What's wrong?"

Jim let out a long sigh and leaned back in his chair. "This whole operation is always on my mind."

"Comes with the territory, Jim. You know that as well as I do."

Jim put his elbow on the desk and grabbed a fistful of hair. "I know, I know."

"Anyway, I just called to let you know that I'm scheduled to speak to the Joint Chiefs in a couple of days. I'd like to hang out with you if that's okay?"

Jim's spirits lifted. He wanted to see his old friend.

"That's great, Ed. I'd love to spend time with you. You can stay at my place if you'd like."

"That'd be great, old chap. You got something else on your mind? I sense something else is bothering you."

"Well, I'm dealing with trying to get the church family to safety. I'd like to talk to you about sending the bulk of the commandos to Saint-Nazaire right away and just stagger them on the ferry every three hours instead of once a day. We need this operation to kick into high gear."

"What made you shift your thinking?"

"Kramer is back."

"Oh, dear God! I didn't know. I thought he had moved on."

"That was our hope. Now Spangler won't be able to help us much."

"Well, that does throw a wrinkle in our plans. I'll contact Bermuda and have them wind down the training. I think those guys are ready to go now."

"Thanks, Ed. It's actually made me feel better to talk to you."

"I'll see you tomorrow, old friend."

Jim hung up the phone and actually smiled. He felt better about things, and he was going to get to see his friend. Jim started typing a message on his Enigma machine:

Will try to get better communications for the troops under your command. Happy about McLaughton. He will be a big help to you. Sending the other commandos your way ASAP. More later.

Jim put away his machine and stood up. He walked to the window, crossed his arms, and smiled. It seemed that events were turning in the right direction.

CHAPTER 16

The church family had made it to the edge of the woods outside of Saint-Malo-de-Guersac. The signal to stop—a fist in the air—came from the front. It was quiet. It would have been better if there was at least a breeze blowing to create background sounds, but it was deathly still. The town was sleeping, at least for the most part. Some of the homes had lamps lit in the windows. It had been so long since Alexandre had seen a real home with electricity that he gasped.

After the commandos in the lead were satisfied that the coast was clear, they gave the signal to move. About halfway down the block, there was an old, abandoned warehouse. The families climbed up on the docks and entered the opening between two doors that had become rotten and fallen off. The center of the room was lit only by the moonlight from outside. The corners of the room were dark.

The families were happy to find dark corners, and most had collapsed on the bags of clothes to sleep. The bags were excellent temporary mattresses for the exhausted bunch. The commando team was also exhausted, but someone had to stand watch. They flipped a coin to see who would be the first, and Peter lost the toss.

Josephine pulled a few clothes from couple of the sacks, and Alexandre was trying to make Sophie and Alise comfortable, and then he checked on others to help them get them situated. Emma laid down next to her mother and wiggled back until she was snuggled in tightly against her. Josephine draped her arm over Emma.

"Do you remember our talk?"

Emma knew exactly what Mother was referring to. "Yes, Mother. I remember."

"You should be proud of your husband. He sacrificed his wedding night to make sure the ones he loves were safe."

A tear rolled out of Emma's eye, and she realized that she had been selfish. "I know, Mother. I am proud of Bill."

"You've got a good man, dear. Just like I've got a good man for a husband. You're lucky that you have that man for a father."

Emma wished for her perch. She longed for her place to think and mourn. She longed for the time she had spent being held by Bill as they gazed at the stars. She remembered the times they talked—and the times words weren't necessary. Emma embraced her mother's arm in a tight hug and cried herself to sleep.

The nightmare was always the same, with minor tweaks here and there. Once again, Bill woke and bolted upright. He was sweating.

Henry was kneeling beside him with a concerned look on his face. "Still having those nightmares, buddy?"

Bill was not completely awake, and the visions of a fireball were still echoing in his brain.

"I'm awake. I'm awake," Bill said, panting.

"It's okay, Bill. You're okay now."

Bill wiped his face with the lapel on his shirt. "I just wish I could figure out this nightmare."

"Care to talk about it?"

Bill didn't really want to talk about it, but Henry already knew the main details, so he decided to fill Henry in on the changes.

"The nightmare isn't always the same anymore. There's still all the fire and blah blah blah." Bill paused and shook his head. "But there are a few things that have changed. I hear a voice in the background that says, 'Lead the target.' I don't recognize the voice."

"Is that the only change?" Henry asked.

"No. I see the demon in the fireball moving its mouth, and I hear the word *well*. That's where the nightmare ends."

Henry wrinkled his face in thought. He slowly shook his head.

"The phrase 'lead the target' we learned in training for the bombers," Henry said.

Bill and Henry both knew that in battle, the gunners needed to fire ahead of the moving targets so that the bullets wouldn't trail behind the target. It's a skill that's learned from experience. Distance? Rate of speed? Firing directly at a target was just a waste of bullets.

Bill shook his head very quickly as if he were clearing cobwebs.

"Enough about me. You need to get some sleep!"

"I'll sleep when I'm dead."

"You'll be dead from lack of sleep. Now get some rest, tough guy!"

Bill pointed to the floor, and Henry put up both hands.

"Okay! Okay! You don't have to be so bossy!"

"And, Henry?"

"Yeah, Bill?"

"It's good to see you again!"

Henry stuck his thumb up in the air.

"You too, Mr. Waist Gunner."

Saint-Malo-de-Guersac, July 23, 1943, 0400

Alexandre was roused from his short amount of sleep by voices. He looked toward the opening and saw two of the commandos talking to someone outside the door. Alexandre rolled off the bags and onto the floor and started moving toward the source of the conversation.

"Good morning, Mr. Bellerose," said Peter.

"Good morning," Alexandre said.

Alexandre would be having a better morning if he had a cup of coffee in his hand. It's one of the luxuries that he was going to miss—at least for now.

"Pardon my intrusion, gentlemen. What do we have here?"

"One very sweet little lady," replied Paul Hightower, the British commando, "and she's brought a dish of breakfast."

The sweet little lady appeared to be in her eighties, and she had a very sincere smile.

"I'm Alexandre Bellerose," Alexandre said as he smiled.

"I'm Jeanne Brodeur. I live across the street with my husband."

"It's so nice to make your acquaintance. Would one of you gentlemen take the tray?"

Peter took the tray and just stood there and held it.

Alexandre stepped off the dock and shook Mrs. Brodeur's hand.

"This was a very nice thing you did. We appreciate your help."

"I saw you people, and you looked tired and hungry. Are you refugees?"

"Yes. We're from Saint-Nazaire. We were living in the old ruined church there after the destruction."

Mrs. Brodeur covered her mouth with her hand, and her eyes turned pink. She had begun to tear up.

"I wasn't aware that anyone had survived that tragedy."

"There are twenty-six of us who actually survived. Now we've been run out of the church by the Nazis."

Mrs. Brodeur was heartbroken to hear this news, and tears ran down her face. She told Alexandre that she was glad that so many had survived the bombing on that fateful night in 1941.

"We've had to survive on our own for two years, so we're accustomed to the problems."

"I'm so sorry that you've had such a bad time. We were invaded, and some of our people were killed, but the Nazis don't really pay much attention to us. This is a really quiet town."

"I'm sorry that you had to lose anyone, Mrs. Brodeur. I know the feeling of losing people who are dear to you."

By this time, a small group of neighbors had begun their day and had wandered over to the warehouse to see what was happening. No one else in the neighborhood had noticed the refugees arriving.

The families inside the warehouse were awakened by the voices and were slowly getting out of their makeshift beds and wandering over to the door.

The neighbors were truly horrified by the sight of the haggard refugees, and some were weeping openly.

CHAPTER 17

"I've got to get that church destroyed!" Kramer said.

"It's already in ruins, sir," replied Spangler.

Kramer looked at Spangler with contempt. Before him was the very man who had undermined him by sending the Jews away instead of giving Kramer the satisfaction of killing them himself.

"It's not smoldering!" screamed Kramer.

Spangler stepped back, pretty sure that he didn't want to say anything else.

"In all fairness, sir, we saved ourselves a lot of trouble with disposing of the bodies."

Spangler was hoping that this explanation had appeased Kramer, but he knew that the demonic mind would find a way to explode with a flurry of insults.

"I should have disposed of your body long ago, Spangler."

Surprisingly, Kramer calmed down, and Spangler didn't get the butt end of his anger. It was odd, so Spangler walked past the desk where Kramer was seated to get a glimpse of what had taken his attention.

"If you don't mind me asking, what are you working on, sir?"

"We've been informed that we'll be getting a shipment of some material we removed from an American ship we captured. Something that those weakling Allies call *napalm*." Kramer squinted at the print.

"And how do we handle this ... napalm, sir?"

"We'll store it on the west dock for now. It'll be here in two days." Kramer sat back in his chair. "I hope I can count on you to deal with protecting it. I can't count on you for much less!" Back in the old days, Kramer's words and tone would have offended Spangler. But he had become so accustomed to being berated and insulted that it was actually a compliment that Kramer would trust him at all.

"I'm going out to the west dock. Try not to screw anything up while I'm gone." He stood up and made his way out.

Spangler waited a few seconds before he sat down at the desk and retrieved his Enigma machine.

Washington, DC, 1045 Local Time

Jim had just picked up Ed at Washington National Airport, and they were winding their way out of the parking lot back up to the highway.

"It's good to see you, Ed."

"I'm glad to be here, Jim," said Ed as he sifted through his briefcase. Ed retrieved a pack of papers.

"We've got a little problem I need to discuss with you," Jim said.

"Oh? It doesn't surprise me that there are problems. It's a way of life, it would seem."

Ed looked away from the papers and glanced at Jim over the top of his reading glasses. "You look thoughtful, old friend."

Jim shook his head and sighed.

"I got word from the initial team that they may have been found out." Jim relayed the details of what Henry had sent via Enigma.

"It doesn't really matter if they know the initial team is there. They have no idea that forty-five more commandos are on the way. The few patrols the Nazis have afforded is appalling for them and will be an advantage for us."

"I think this operation is going to be the death of me," Jim said.

"Nah. It'll make you stronger." They arrived at the Pentagon but were still sitting in the car.

"So, what's the update on the remaining commandos?"

"They've left Bermuda and are on their way to London by plane."

"The operation will commence in ten days?"

"Yes. We can finally get this behind us."

Saint-Malo-de-Guersac

Emma sat on the porch swing of the Brodeur home. All five of the families had been taken in by different households in the very friendly town, and that was consoling her. They had been fed, and they now had access to a doctor when they had health concerns.

The kitchens in the five homes were always bustling with the ladies of the church families doing their share of the cooking and cleaning. The men helped with repairs and general chores around and about the town. The children played with the other children in the neighborhood. Most of the children were too young to remember what it was like to meet different people, and they seemed to be adjusting well to their new environment.

All this activity should have made Emma happy, but her happiness was blocked. The one true love in her life was not by her side. The only consolation that she had from that was the fact that he was off defending her and their family. Somehow, that didn't seem like much of a consolation. She was lonely even though she was surrounded by people.

The people of the town had treated the families not as refugees but as their own. The commandos had returned to the plane, and Emma wished that she had at least asked to accompany them. She knew that her father would never approve, but she could have at least asked.

Her thoughts were interrupted by Alexandre stepping out the front door. He saw Emma sitting alone.

"May I join you, dear?"

"You know I always want you near me, Father."

Alexandre stepped over to the swing and sat next to Emma. He put his arm around her and began to gently rock the swing back and forth.

"I know you really miss Bill, dear."

"I do miss him, Father."

"This will all be over with one day, and you'll be together and bring me many grandchildren." He pulled her tighter.

Emma put her head on her father's chest and sighed. No words would ever be enough to describe her anguish over not being with her true love. "Please show me a way I can see him again."

Alexandre looked off into the distance as he did when he was going to bestow some sort of clairvoyant wisdom. When Alexandre spoke, everyone listened. He had always been a bellwether when it came to destiny.

"You'll see him again soon. I can promise you that. I can see an egg with raised squares and a silver spout growing out of the top of it." Emma was confused. *What was Father referring to?* She listened intently as her father continued.

"Don't mourn. Rejoice and be glad. Your destiny is with your husband who is now my son. He's going to make many people very proud and very safe."

Emma was even more confused than before, but strangely enough, she had found solace in his words. Alexandre started to leave the swing, and Emma held onto him. "Sit with me for a bit longer, Father."

Alexandre smiled as he sat back in the swing.

Bill was woken by the sound of footsteps outside. He reached in his pocket, retrieved his pistol, and stood up next to the opening. When the men stepped through the door, they were met with a drawn pistol.

"Whoa! Easy, old chap," James said.

"Whew! That was a rude awakening," Bill said.

The men laughed. They spent the next few minutes explaining the situation with the church families and how they were now safe. The story gave Bill some peace of mind.

"You need to go see your wife, Bill," Henry said.

"I need to be here to protect my wife," Bill said.

"You haven't had a proper honeymoon, my friend. I insist that you go to her."

Bill thought on this for a moment and then bobbed his head up and down. "I'll go see her, but I'll make it a short trip. I need to be here."

"In case you hadn't realized it, Sergeant, I'm the lieutenant here," Henry said.

"You know I've been declared dead, Lieutenant?"

Bill sighed. He looked at Henry with resignation and then grumbled, "Okay, Lieutenant, I'll follow orders to the letter of the law."

Bill said this phrase sarcastically, and the other men looked on in dismay. They thought that just maybe Henry was going to reprimand Bill for his sarcasm.

"Get out of here, Bill—and don't come back for at least forty-eight hours."

"Yes, sir," Bill said as he saluted.

The salute was sincere. Bill exited the plane and began his journey to see Emma and his new family.

Washington, DC, July 24, 1943, 1100 Local Time

Jim Mason and Edward Davies had just entered the War Room at the Pentagon and were seated in the "hot seats" in front of the audience.

"This should be easy enough," Jim said.

"I'm not a bit concerned about it. I'm British, remember? Diplomatic immunity and all that tommy rot?"

The Joint Chiefs of Staff filed in and took their seats on the panel.

The chairman asked, "First item on the agenda?"

"Operation Saint-Nazaire, sir," the clerk said with his usual official cadence.

The chairman said, "I see we have an update, gentlemen. Mr. Jim Mason and Mr. Edward Davies. We've got the best of both worlds."

There was a short eruption of laughter.

"Mr. Davies, so glad you could make it. Do you have an agenda for us?"

A young intern had already made his way to pick up the packet of information that Jim and Ed had worked on overnight. He took the paperwork up to the chairman who put on his reading glasses and began to examine it.

"You can begin anytime, Mr. Davies. I can read and listen at the same time, which is something my wife would disagree with."

There was another short burst of laughter.

Ed said, "Well, sir, we've got an issue with some napalm that was confiscated from an Allied ship by a school of German patrol boats."

"We've been made painfully aware of that, Mr. Davies. Is there a plan to get this material back?"

"No, sir. We have an alternative to reacquiring the material. We have included this material in our plans for the big bang—if you'll pardon the expression. Napalm is highly incendiary and will burn for a long time. We'll have to wait to see exactly where they put the drums before we can formulate a further plan."

"And the families are safe now?"

"Yes, sir. They've already found homes in Saint-Malo-de-Guersac. They are being well taken care of, sir."

"I'm glad to hear that, Mr. Davies. There was a concern about creating collateral damage."

"Yes, sir. It's actually worked out better than we expected."

"We'll wait for your reports on the ongoing operation, gentlemen."

Saint-Malo-de-Guersac, July 24, 1943, 1630 Local Time

Bill had made it to the city of Saint-Malo-de-Guersac and stood at the edge of the forest. He looked around, and it seemed to be quiet. No Nazi soldiers were in sight. As he walked down the street, he saw the warehouse on the right. He knew that his new family lived in a house across the street with a nice elderly couple.

Emma had stepped out of the house after assisting with the dinner dishes and took her seat back on the porch swing. This swing was a far cry from what she had called her "perch," but it would do. Just as long as she had a place to think, she was fine. She closed her eyes and thought of how much she wanted to be with Bill. Her wedding night had been a disaster, and she wanted him next to her.

"Care for some company?" came a familiar voice.

Emma opened her eyes quickly.

Bill stood smiling before her with his arms outstretched.

Emma began to weep tears of joy.

Bill knelt before her and put his arms around her.

Emma put her hands on his face and had begun to breathe quickly in anticipation of the kiss that was sure to happen.

Bill kissed her very passionately for what seemed to be a short while, when in fact it was at least two minutes. The kiss ended, and Bill held her very tightly.

She had her chin on his shoulder, and her arms were wrapped in a strong grip around his head.

He grasped her tightly around her back.

Emma wept tears of pure joy.

Bill began massaging a circle on her back, and Emma was enjoying the feeling of his touch.

"I love you so much," Emma said in a breathless whisper.

"You are my heart. I will love you always!" Bill said as he lightly kissed her shoulder.

They heard the front door open and realized from past experience that they would never actually be able to have a private moment.

"I'm sorry. I didn't mean to interrupt."

Bill stood up, and Emma lowered her head in embarrassment.

"It's good to see you, Mother!" Bill said as he put his arms around her.

"I didn't know you were here. I'll get you some food."

They entered the house, and there were quite a few people in the living room. Bill was introduced to the Brodeurs.

Mr. Brodeur was sitting in his recliner and appeared to be a tiny and very frail man. Bill gently took his hand and introduced himself.

Bill made his way to the kitchen where Josephine had prepared him a plate of food. Emma joined him at the table.

"Remember when I used to feed you?" Emma asked with a sly smile.

"How could I ever forget that? You were so nervous. It was cute," Bill said.

"Me? What about you? You were stumbling all over your words. I thought you were mentally challenged!" Emma put her hands on her hips.

They both laughed.

Emma linked her left arm with Bill's right as he enjoyed his meal.

"Do you know that I'm right-handed?"

"I know that. I just want all your attention. Your right arm is my best bet."

Bill made the best of eating with his left hand and spilled most of the food back onto the plate.

Emma said. "Should I feed you?"

"Hmm. Interesting idea. I'd like you to feed me your lips."

"That can be arranged, Mr. McLaughton."

"I'm sure it can be, Mrs. McLaughton."

Washington, DC, July 24, 1943, 1215 Local Time

"Look at this," Jim said as he handed a small packet of papers to Ed.

Ed took the papers. The pair had decided to work out of Jim's office at the Pentagon to put some finer touches on Operation Saint-Nazaire.

"Yes. It looks like Spangler has come through for us again. The drums are arriving in a few hours, and he's provided us with exact locations set aside for storage." Ed squinted at the page. "Since the drums will be on the west dock, we can spare the east dock for the commandos to escape."

"Yes. And the smoke from the napalm will supply a good cover for that escape," Jim said.

"I see the last message from Spangler says that Kramer wants to test out the napalm on human subjects."

"Yes, I saw that. He's nothing but pure evil!" Jim said, gritting his teeth.

"Spangler has stuck his neck out for this operation."

"He's been a good ally. Too bad he wasn't born an ally."

"It's only a matter of time before he's found out. I would really hate to be in his shoes when that happens!"

"He's come too far to turn back now."

"We still need him. If he's found out before the operation is complete, we'll be in trouble. We won't get any more help from him."

"We'll have to cross that bridge when we get there. We can only hope that he doesn't get found out." Jim sighed and shook his head.

Saint-Nazaire

The commando crew had repaired the right waist gun and were in the process of clearing a few trees from the window next to it. Slowly and quietly, they worked. The trees would be moved toward the tail of the plane so that tents could be set up to house the commandos while they prepared for the operation. There would also be trees cleared from the left side since it provided a great deal more cover.

The men had made two raids on the cove to recover more equipment, and they had not encountered any opposition in the process. The operation was well into preparation as five more commandos had arrived. Through the efforts and aid of Spangler, the operation was proceeding as planned.

Henry had received a message on the Enigma, and it was indeed troubling. Jim had told him about the napalm and the need for the destruction of the material. In the meantime, General Major Josef Kramer would be experimenting with human subjects.

The last haul of equipment from the cove included a number of Bren light machine guns, flashlights, walkie-talkies, food, two hundred pounds of plastic explosives, and two large bags of ammunition for the machine guns. The plastic explosives would be used to detonate the bombs in the bomb bay. In order to achieve the detonation, they would have to disarm the safety devices on the bombs, but that would be a last-minute detail.

Henry stepped outside to survey the work, and it made him think of the night the operation was set to unfold. It was going to be a big deal, and so much was set to happen. Timing was going to be key. Underwater operations were to detonate two hundred pounds of plastics that were set to blast the U-boat pens and uproot the submarine nets. The divers would start at the cove and work their way one quarter of a mile—loaded with fifty pounds of plastic each—to the docks. Hopefully, there would be enough ships in the repair docks to justify the damage intention.

It was all about timing and no one being captured in the operation.

"God help us," Henry said as he looked toward the docks.

Spangler said, "The ship has arrived, sir."

Kramer said, "Good. How many drums?"

"There are more than we thought. Maybe five hundred?"

Kramer smiled. He had some new toys—not only for death but also for torture and experiments. He was truly a demon. There was no one in his past, except his mother, who could ever say they loved him, and no one was ever loved by this evil being. He had never been married, and he never intended to get married. As far as he was concerned, every human was scum, except for himself, of course. "Is there equipment to spray the napalm?"

"Yes, sir."

"Good. Get me the equipment and save a drum for me. I'll need to *test* the merchandise." This comment made Spangler's skin crawl. As much as Kramer hated him, it was in his mind that Kramer might want to use him for his experiments. The night of the operation couldn't come soon enough. He was prepared to die, and if he were to die in battle, then all the better. Maybe death would be quick. Anyway, death would be better than the stress that he'd brought on himself.

"Spangler!" Kramer yelled and snapped his fingers.

"Yes, sir?"

"Pay attention to me!"

"I'm sorry, sir. I have a lot on my mind."

"The only thing you have on your mind is what I tell you!"

"Again, I apologize, sir."

Kramer scowled at Spangler.

"Is there something you wanted to tell me, sir?"

"You've got more on your mind than the business at hand."

"I'm just not feeling well, sir," said Spangler.

He hoped this lie would draw some of the anger off him and back to the business at hand.

"Now, where were we?" growled Kramer.

"We were discussing the use of the napalm, sir."

Kramer's grin was devilish.

"Ah, yes," said Kramer and drifted off in a daydream.

Spangler stepped over to the big picture window and folded his arms across his chest, as usual.

Saint-Malo-de-Guersac

At dusk, Bill and Emma made a makeshift bed in the shed behind the Brodeur home.

Emma said, "What are you thinking about, dear?"

"The little pact we made about you going to the bomber."

"I know. It was bad timing. It's not your fault."

"Now it'll never happen. There are too many soldiers there."

"Again. It's not your fault."

Bill put his arms around his new bride.

Emma moved closer to Bill. They were nose to nose, and she was longing for a kiss. Bill made that wish come true and kissed her passionately. His left hand moved to her thigh, and he stroked her up and down.

Emma moaned in anticipation of more action waiting in the wings.

Bill left her lips and began to kiss her chin. He made nice circles of little snips of kisses all around it.

Emma closed her eyes and sighed heavily. She put her hand on the back of his head and began to massage his hair. She occasionally grabbed a fistful.

Bill moved back to her lips and kissed her very deeply. He traveled back down to her chin and worked his way to her neck.

Emma tilted her head back to give Bill more access to every part of it.

He nibbled down her neck and further down to her chest. He began to unbutton her shirt as her breathing quickened.

Alexandre was drinking coffee with Josephine and Mr. and Mrs. Brodeur.

Abraham Brodeur was eighty-five. He was disabled and needed help to do most anything that didn't involve sitting in his recliner. It was good to have his company at the dinner table that night.

"So, how was your day, Alexandre?"

Alexandre paused for a moment as he reflected on the day's events.

"Well, I saw something that didn't look right," replied Alexandre.

The ladies took a break in their conversation to listen to what Alexandre was about to reveal.

Alexandre continued.

"I saw a convoy of trucks. They had Nazi markings on them. The last truck looked like it had bars on the windows. A really frail-looking individual was holding onto the bars and looking out at me."

The ladies both put their hands to their mouths and started to tear up.

The men also knew what it meant, and they were silent for several minutes. Alexandre finally broke the silence.

"I don't know how many were in the truck. I know they were headed toward Saint-Nazaire, possibly going to the docks to either be workers or maybe worse."

Everyone at the table knew what the word "worse" meant.

"I'll have a talk with Bill about it. He can get word to the crew—and maybe they can do something to help those poor people."

CHAPTER 18

Henry had seen the convoy pass by on the road just two miles west of their position and had grabbed his binoculars. The convoy entered the east dock, except for the last truck. Henry adjusted the binoculars to zoom in as close as he could on the truck that had stopped, and he recognized it as a prisoner transport truck. The bars on the windows were a dead giveaway. He also noticed two people holding onto the bars and looking out.

A short time later, a man in an officer's uniform got into the passenger's side of the truck, and another truck exited the dock. The second truck had equipment loaded on it: a drum and what Henry recognized as a flamethrower.

"James, come with me," Henry said.

"Yes, sir."

The two men grabbed Bren light machine guns and set out through the woods to investigate what was happening with the prisoner truck.

Fifteen minutes later, they arrived at an embankment and moved quietly to the top. As they got to the rise, they peered over and saw a group of soldiers who had assembled along with the trucks. The two prisoners were herded out of one truck and tied to trees. The poor souls were so rail thin that it didn't seem possible that they were even alive. They were standing on their own, but barely.

The Nazi officer exited the passenger seat of the transport and picked up the flamethrower. Two soldiers attached the hose to the drum, and another lit the equipment. The officer didn't hesitate to pull the trigger, and out spewed a large amount of flame. The flames engulfed the men tied to the trees. Their screams were unbearable.

The officer barked orders at the soldiers, and Henry focused his binoculars on his face. It was Kramer. There was no doubt about it.

Henry wanted to kill Kramer then and there, but unfortunately, he couldn't make a scene. Exposing himself would be a death knell for the operation.

The bodies continued to burn until even the bones were turning to ashes.

Kramer got back in the truck, and they departed the area. Henry put his binoculars back in their pouch and shook his head.

"We have to get back, James."

"Yes, sir," said James who was obviously sickened by what he had witnessed.

The walk back to the bomber was silent.

Saint-Malo-de-Guersac

The time had come for Bill to return to Saint-Nazaire, and the tears had already begun. The usual banter had started about Bill having to leave and Emma's desire to follow him. It was the same old story.

"You knew I would have to leave, dear," Bill said.

"And you knew I was going to want to go back with you."

"And you knew I was going to tell you that it was too dangerous," Bill said as he rolled his eyes. "This argument it starting to circle."

"It was worth the effort," Emma said, frowning in disappointment.

Bill kissed her gently, and then he hugged Josephine. He grabbed his backpack and made his way out the front door.

The walk back to Saint-Nazaire would take just over two hours, and Bill was excited to get back to help Henry and the commandos. He was not trained as a commando, but he had the resolve to stop the Nazis and the evil general major.

Many thoughts crossed Bill's mind as he made his journey, including thoughts of Emma and her stubborn mind. She was young and had a mind of her own, and he hoped she wouldn't follow him back into danger. He hoped her reasoning would override her stubbornness.

There were so many things that he still didn't know about his new wife. He was in love with her, and he would give his life to save her, but he hoped she wouldn't put herself in a position that would cause him to have to protect her. "Stay in your safe place," Bill said to no one in particular.

Saint-Nazaire

"You should have been there, Spangler!" Kramer said.

Spangler knew what Kramer was talking about, and he was physically sickened by the thought of what had occurred in the forest.

"You know I'm busy here, sir."

Spangler was hoping that Kramer wouldn't regale him with the specifics of the torture that had unfolded.

"If only we had a way to make a movie out of the screams and the agony," Kramer said gleefully. "But unfortunately, we don't have that kind of equipment here."

A look of dejection crossed Kramer's face as he mourned not being able to relive the torture and death of the individuals who had been unlucky enough to have been selected for the barbaric action. This was barbarism at its worst, and that was Kramer's cup of tea. Demonic and barbaric!

"Maybe it will be possible one day, sir," said Spangler insincerely.

"If only I could get a camera crew here," said Kramer in deep and serious contemplation.

Spangler was truly horrified at the thought of Kramer frying more human bodies. He tried desperately not to let his facial expressions display his thoughts. Spangler had put up with a lot of Kramer's evil ways, but this was new territory, and Spangler was close to panic as he thought of ways to stop the barbarism.

"I'll talk to Herr Hitler himself if I have to. The Third Reich needs to get in on the fun."

The word "fun" turned Spangler's stomach.

"I need to get over to the west dock, sir. I want to make sure that the unloading of the drums is going smoothly," said Spangler, hoping Kramer would buy his excuse for leaving his presence.

"I'll be leaving tonight to go to Berlin. I have to get to the Third Reich to pitch my idea."

Bill arrived at the bomber, entered the fuselage, and saw Henry tapping on the Enigma machine.

Henry looked up and nodded with no smile for Bill.

"Got something on your mind, brother? You seem to be concerned about something," Bill said as he sat on a box.

"Yeah. I witnessed something that I wish I'd never seen." Henry lowered and shook his head.

Henry relayed the sight that he had seen, and Bill grimaced as he heard of the deaths of the men by the hands of Kramer.

"I wanted to kill that bastard!" Henry said, gritting his teeth in anger.

"We're on the same sheet of music with that one. Kramer is the one who ordered the overkill on the city just below us. He nearly killed the love of my life and her family," Bill said.

Henry was still scowling as many thoughts raced through his mind. He felt complete despair and a sense of failure that he could do nothing to help anyone, at least not until the operation was in full swing.

"I've just sent a message to the OSS, I guess in an attempt to possibly get some advisement on this situation," Henry said in despair.

"We can only do what we can do, brother. I don't mean to minimize the importance of protecting the innocent, but we have our hands tied here," Bill said.

Henry nodded in agreement.

The waist gun had been repaired, and the trees outside had been arranged in such a manner that they could be cleared with a simple detonation. A small number of plastic explosives had been buried beneath the outer rim of trees, and one blast would clear them at the touch of a button. It would be very handy when it came time to lead the Nazi soldiers up the hill in pursuit. They would never know what hit them when the waist gun blared and killed a large number of them.

Washington, DC

Jim and Ed had just gone over the activities of the day and had been presented with the messages from Spangler and Henry.

Jim looked at Ed in contemplation. "I need you to extend your stay for a while," Jim said rather dryly.

"How long did you have to think about that?"

"I'm out of my league, Ed."

"I'll stay, Jim. But it's because I know you need help. It's not because I think you're inexperienced but rather because it will be easier for us to communicate without having to shout messages across the pond."

Jim chuckled.

"And besides, I don't want to miss out on that fine cooking from June," said Ed as he patted his stomach.

Jim chuckled again because he knew Ed was right. June was Jim's wife, and yes, she was a very good cook. She and Ed got along famously, and she wouldn't mind an extended stay of their close friend. "I'm going to have to tell Henry that he can't help those people. That's going to be difficult for Henry and me."

Ed leaned forward and said, "We have to do it this way, Jim. Remember that conversation you had with General Hinckley?"

"I do."

"A few lives will have to be sacrificed—unfortunately—but many more lives will be saved in the long run."

Jim was somewhat comforted, but not totally so. He would still grieve for the losses of not only the lives of civilians but also the lives of the Allied soldiers.

"I just wish we could move up the operation," Jim said.

"We only have twenty commandos on the site—and trying to carry out such an intense operation with less than half the crew is suicide."

Jim knew that Ed was right. He realized that trying to rush the operation to completion was selfish. He wanted to be rid of the Nazi stranglehold and the thoughts of people dying because of plans that he had helped make.

"Let's go get some lunch, buddy," said Ed with a forced smile.

Jim nodded.

Saint-Malo-de-Guersac

Alexandre stood in the field as he leaned on his hoe and watched the convoy of trucks headed to Saint-Nazaire. He counted fifteen trucks, four of which had bars for windows and more rail-thin people clinging to them. He felt sorry for the people, but there was nothing he could do about it. Alexandre furrowed his brow in deep sorrow and went back to work.

— ⚓ —

Emma sat at the dinner table with her mother and Jeanne Brodeur, which was the usual place to find the two older ladies. As for Emma, not so much. Maybe she just needed the closeness of other people. She knew that Bill had to leave, and maybe she was taking it harder than she expected.

"You're missing Bill," Josephine said.

It wasn't a question, it was a statement, and it puzzled Emma.

"Yes. I'm missing Bill. I'll always miss him when he's not near me," Emma replied. Her face displayed her puzzlement.

"Do you find it odd that I would know that?" asked Josephine, sensing Emma's confusion.

Emma knew that her mother was not stupid, and that she had experienced the same feelings that Emma now felt. "It's not odd, Mother. I can remember how sad you were when Father was away on business," she replied with a sympathetic look.

She took her mother's hand, as if to comfort her, but the fact was that it was Emma who needed comfort.

"I miss him so much," Emma said. A tear appeared in her left eye, and slowly trickled down her face.

Josephine glanced at Jeanne, and Jeanne closed her eyes and nodded one slow nod. Josephine took this to mean that Jeanne was excusing herself from the table. As Jeanne rose to leave, she touched Emma on the shoulder in a consoling sort of way and then exited the room.

"You're in pain, and I don't like to see you this way," Josephine said.

"I suppose I need to learn to deal with it."

"It's not so much that you need to deal with it. It's more about having patience than it is anything else."

"Patience?"

"What I'm trying to say is that you need to wait on Bill. Don't try to speed things up."

Emma was now totally confused. She had no idea what her mother was trying to tell her. Josephine could see by the look on Emma's face that she didn't understand her meaning, so she tried to simplify it for her.

"Don't go to Bill. Wait on him here. He's in danger, and he doesn't need you there to slow him down. I was trying to keep from having to say that because I knew it would hurt your feelings."

Emma thought on this for a moment, and then she replied, "If Bill is in grave danger, I'll go to him to try to save him. Death for us both is better than being a widow."

Josephine gasped and covered her mouth. She had not expected to hear Emma say what she did. Josephine just sat for a moment, unsure of how to respond to this statement. Had Emma's love for Bill blinded her to the need for her own safety?

"I'm sure you'll do the right thing when the time comes," Josephine said after a long pause.

"My husband is trying to protect us. The very least I can do is offer my support in this effort. I know you don't agree—and you feel that maybe I've lost my mind—but I think it's the right thing to do."

Josephine was in deep distress. She knew she'd have to have a talk with Alexandre. He'd know how to handle this situation. So many things were on Josephine's mind that she didn't even notice that tears had started to trickle down her cheeks. Emma knew that her words had hurt her mother, something she didn't mean to do. Emma stood, put her arms around Josephine, and kissed her on top of her head.

"I'm going to help protect my family, Mother. I would certainly hope that you would understand that."

Saint-Nazaire

Henry picked up his binoculars and watched the trucks approaching the west dock.

Bill moved up beside him and pulled his binoculars from the pouch on his side.

"Same thing as last time?" asked Bill as he fumbled with the focus.

"Yep. But there are more prisoners this time. Looks like four prison containers."

"Good chance we need to do something," Bill replied.

"We've been instructed to stay out of it." Henry lowered the binoculars and shook his head.

"And you're okay with that?"

Henry looked at Bill. He wasn't sure what was on Bill's mind, but he was hoping that he had not decided to go rogue.

"I'm not okay with it," Henry said after a short pause.

Bill thought for a moment. "You know I'm not one of the designated members of this team. Don't get me wrong. I am dedicated to the operation, but I'm not under orders from the higher-ups. They barely know I exist."

Henry put his binoculars back down on his chest and sighed.

"What would you suggest?"

"I don't know. I don't want to buck against your authority, but I know that I want to help those people."

Henry seemed to be in pain as he thought on the situation. He'd seen the evil that had unfolded, and he wanted desperately to be able to do something to help. These people didn't deserve the demonic evil that awaited them. Henry drew in a deep breath.

"Go do your reconnaissance and report back to me. You've already been seen once by Kramer, so if you're seen again, it won't give us away. He still won't know we're here."

"Yes, sir," replied Bill, saluting. The salute was genuine.

Spangler stood on the east dock and watched the transport boat depart. Kramer was on board, and Spangler was happy to be rid of him for a couple of days. He had been made painfully aware of the fate of the prisoners in the trucks that had just arrived. Spangler knew that he'd have to do something about that.

Bill had supplied himself with a Bren light machine gun and a spare chain of ammo. It was just dusk, and he knew that the Nazi patrol increased at this time of the evening. He charcoaled his face, donned a ski cap, and took out a two-way radio. He needed to maintain radio silence, but he might need to warn the team.

Spangler stood at his window with his arms folded across his chest, as usual. He was in deep thought. If he released the prisoners, where would they go? They were sure to be caught by the patrols. He knew he couldn't just stand by and do nothing. He'd just have to go to them and figure out a plan as events unfolded. He reached in his bottom desk drawer and retrieved his holster strap and a Luger and pulled the strap tightly around his waist.

Bill made his way out of the bomber and moved into the thick tree line beyond the drag marks from where the bomber had crashed. He had never been more determined to carry out an operation. Flying the bomber and bombing places that he had never seen and fighting against people he didn't know was much different than what he was about to attempt. There would be faces attached to the operation, which made him nervous.

Spangler made his way to the west dock, and the soldiers saluted him as he passed the guard shack.

"Do you require an escort, sir?" a guard asked.

"No. I need you to go check on the drums in the storage area."

"Yes, sir." The guard saluted.

Spangler stepped into the guard shack and turned off the floodlights. He then proceeded to walk toward the prisoners in the trucks.

Bill had made his way to the edge of the tree line and had moved to the trucks. He wasn't sure what he was going to do once he got there. He felt a gnawing dread as he imagined being found out. Not only would he lose his life, but he would have failed in rescuing the Jews. He approached the first truck and climbed up the running board and looked in. It was dark, and he didn't dare use his flashlight.

Suddenly there was a voice behind him.

"Can I help you in some way?"

Bill was startled, to say the least. He wheeled around with his machine gun leveled at the source of the voice. It was the officer he had seen the night of the warning. Spangler recognized Bill, and he folded his arms across his chest.

"Bill?"

Bill was amazed that he had remembered his name.

"Lieutenant Spangler," Bill said, "are you here as a friend or a foe?"

Bill was embarrassed that he had used that terminology, but what's done was done.

"You can call me Adelbert. I'm, at least somewhat, surprised to see you here. I thought that you had gone with the church families."

Bill didn't dare give away any specifics of the operation. He was sure that Spangler was aware of the plans already, but Spangler would never hear it from him. Bill lowered the machine gun.

"We have to do this quickly. The guard will return to his post any second now, and we don't want to be caught in this situation," said Spangler as he looked behind him.

"We need to herd these people onto one truck. I'm sure you won't mind driving the truck away from here, and I'm equally as sure that you can do a covert tactic of some sort to hide the truck."

Bill nodded.

The two men opened the doors on the four trucks and quickly moved the Jews to one of them. There were twelve Jews in all. Bill was heartbroken to see the condition of their bodies. Most of them were naked except for the tattered cloths they had wrapped around their genitals.

Bill nodded at Spangler who smiled and nodded.

"I'll alert the first guard post to let you through. You won't even have to stop," said Spangler. "Now hurry. We don't want to be caught here."

"What about you, Adelbert?" inquired Bill.

"The envelope on my fate has already been licked and sealed. I'll be dead soon enough."

Bill reached down to his hip, unclipped the two-way radio and handed it to Spangler.

"I can trust you, Adelbert. You may need this radio to contact us."

Spangler nodded and took the radio.

Bill climbed behind the wheel and started the motor. He drove back to the road and started his journey to God only knew where. He had violated orders from Henry, but he was listed as KIA, at least as far as he knew. "So sue me," Bill said to no one in particular.

Spangler had made his way back onto the west dock. He reached inside the guard shack and turned the floodlights back on. The guard had not yet returned, and he counted that as a blessing. He made his way back to his office and over to the big picture window overlooking the main ship-repair docks. He folded his arms across his chest and just stood there.

As Bill approached the checkpoint, the soldiers moved the arm to the upward position and saluted as he passed. Bill shrank in his seat and saluted back in a concealing manner. He breathed a sigh of relief that he had not been caught. At least not yet.

CHAPTER 19

Saint-Malo-de-Guersac

Alexandre and Josephine sat at the dinner table drinking their evening coffee and silently enjoying each other's company. It had been a long day for Alexandre in the fields, and Josephine was troubled by the earlier conversation with Emma. As usual, she was deep in thought. And, as usual, Alexandre watched her as she sat with her brow furrowed, staring at her coffee cup.

"So, how was your day, dear?" inquired Alexandre.

Josephine slowly looked up. "A little troubling."

"I'm all ears."

"I had a conversation with Emma."

"Oh?"

"Yes. She's desperate to go be with Bill."

"Ah. We knew she was going to want to do that all along."

The conversation paused as Alexandre reached across the table to take Josephine's hand. They had had family problems before, and holding hands usually brought comfort to her and a feeling of accomplishment for him. The very moment he took her hand, she smiled.

"You always know how to make me feel better," Josephine said.

"You deserve to feel better."

Emma had already gone to bed when she heard the door creak. Bill and Emma had made their bedroom in the shed out in back of the main house, and it had one of the old-style doors attached to the frame. The door creaked rather loudly when opening and closing. The two had laughed and joked about the sounds it made. Emma was not yet asleep, and she sat upright on the bed at the creak.

"Emma?" whispered Bill.

"Bill? What are you doing here?" asked Emma.

Emma was glad that Bill was there, but she was concerned.

"I've got a problem. I need you to come with me to talk to Father."

Emma swiveled sideways on the bed, pulled up her pants, and ran barefoot to the door. Bill took her by the hand and led her into the house. There they saw Father and Mother sitting at the dining room table.

"Bill? It's a surprise to see you. Especially at this time of night," Alexandre said.

Bill relayed the happenings of the night and that he had a truckload of Jews just inside of the forest line at the edge of town. Alexandre, being the compassionate man that he was, thought quickly.

"We have to go wake Father Ambroise. He can get these people in the church."

Emma went to the shed to get her shoes and then led the way to the house where Father Ambroise was staying, at least for the time being. She and Bill knocked on the door, and a young man dressed in his nightclothes answered.

"What can I help you with?" asked the young man while rubbing his eyes.

"We're so sorry to wake you, sir. We need to see Father Ambroise please. It's urgent!" exclaimed Bill.

The young man hurried back into the house, and less than a minute later, Father Ambroise appeared.

"We're so sorry to wake you, sir. We have a problem," Bill said.

Bill began explaining what he had told Alexandre, and Father Ambroise ran to his bedroom to quickly get dressed. He emerged, and they began a fast walk down the street. They didn't want to run and draw too much attention.

Alexandre was waiting in front of the Brodeur home, and when they got to that point, he joined them.

When they arrived at the prison truck, Bill opened the back door—and everybody peered in. Twelve very thin souls were inside. It was a heartbreaking sight.

Emma covered her mouth and had begun to weep silently.

Father Ambroise started chanting Catholic prayers underneath his breath. "We need to get these people to the church. We also need to round up Rabiah and the town doctor so they can examine them," said Father Ambroise.

"We'll need to gather food. Come with me, Emma," Alexandre said.

After all was said and done, Bill knew that he would have to solve the problem of hiding the truck. But where?

Saint-Nazaire

Spangler was sending messages to the Allies with his Enigma machine. When he heard a knock on the door, he quickly hid the machine. "Yes?"

The door opened, and a guard walked in and saluted. "Permission to speak, sir?"

"Yes. What is it?" said Spangler in an irritated tone.

"Drums are secure, sir. There's only one problem."

"And? Hurry up. I'm busy!"

Spangler didn't enjoy speaking in such an irritated tone, but he had to maintain the level of command that would suggest he was a true Nazi.

"Some of the drums are in the way of the repairs, sir. If I may, I suggest that we move a few of them to another place."

"And where would you … suggest?"

"The east dock, sir. Ten of the drums would be sufficient, in my opinion, sir."

"Do it. Be sure to put them on the far end, toward the beach."

"Yes, sir."

The guard had turned to leave but then paused and turned back around to face Spangler.

"If I may speak again, sir?"

"Make it quick!"

"One of the trucks went missing last night, sir."

"Let that be of no concern to you! Now leave and speak of this to no one!" Spangler growled, trying to interject as much contempt as possible.

The guard saluted and made his exit.

Spangler realized that he had dug his own grave. The missing truck issue was not going to go away, but he had done the right thing, and that's all that mattered. Kramer would be back tomorrow, and he would certainly want Spangler's head for allowing it to happen. Spangler knew that he could flee and make a new life for himself, but he still had work to do to help the Allies.

Forty-five of the fifty commandos had arrived and hidden themselves around the bomber. There were two days until the operation would commence, and that wouldn't be soon enough, in Henry's opinion. Henry was deep in thought, but his thoughts weren't currently on the operation. Bill had not returned or reported in. His absence greatly concerned him. If he had been captured, the patrols would increase exponentially—and Henry would have lost a good friend.

"Lieutenant?" came a voice outside of Henry's thoughts.

Henry snapped out of his own little world and realized that it was James who had called to him.

"Yes?"

"We've just returned from the cove with some new supplies," said James.

As he spoke, four other commandos came in dragging five more bags.

"What kind of haul did you get?" Henry opened the first bag and rifled through it to get a better look.

"We got a few flak jackets—the kind that are used on bomber missions."

"Very good! I want all the men in this camp to wear one at all times."

"Immediately, sir?"

"Yes. Is that a problem?"

"No, sir," said James.

"Good. Put this stuff away."

Henry was concerned about a lot of things, but the safety of the men in his charge was problem number one. If there were more patrols added to the forest, his men would need all the protection that could be afforded. And he was going to make sure they got it.

"You seem distressed, sir," said James.

"What?" Henry said.

"You seem distant, sir. I'm guessing it's a concern for Bill?"

"Your guess would be correct. We can't afford to have this operation fail because of personal feelings toward people outside of the plan."

Henry was referring to the Jewish people, and it pained him to have to say it, but it was the truth. Henry felt a great deal of compassion for the Jewish people, but he also realized that collateral damage would be necessary to carry out saving many more lives in the long run.

"Should we go look for him?" said James.

"No. We can't risk being exposed. And besides, he knew the risks."

James nodded and turned to walk away.

Henry hadn't expected an easy command. In fact, he had anticipated having to make decisions that he really didn't want to make. Leaving his friend without support was one of those decisions.

Saint-Malo-de-Guersac

The Jews had been hurried down the alleyway behind the warehouse and on to the back door of the church.

Alexandre and Emma went home to prepare food with Josephine.

Bill was contemplating how to get the truck hidden, and he decided to take it to the warehouse and hide it beneath the garbage and damaged building materials in a dark corner. There was a ramp on the back side of the warehouse, so it would hopefully simplify the job.

"We can make sandwiches for now," Alexandre said to Josephine and Emma. Jeanne had joined them in the kitchen and hurried to help get more food together. Abraham struggled out of the bedroom with his walker and approached the kitchen.

"You need to be in bed, Abraham!" exclaimed Jeanne with concern in her voice. "You're going to hurt yourself!"

"I'll be fine, honey. I have to help." Abraham sat down at the table and began making sandwiches.

"You're a good man, Abraham!" Alexandre said.

"You're an even better man, Alexandre," Abraham said with a smile.

Alexandre, Josephine, and Emma had been a godsend on many levels for Abraham and Jeanne. Alexandre had provided the food, Josephine had kept the house immaculately clean, and Emma had been good company for Abraham and his wife. She was like a granddaughter. Abraham hoped the Bellerose family would never leave, but alas, that day would come, much to the chagrin of the Brodeur couple.

Bill entered the kitchen, sweating and disheveled, and Emma handed him a towel to dry off and clean up.

"It's a done deal. The truck is hidden," Bill said.

"Good!" Alexandre said as he smiled.

They made up about three dozen sandwiches and packed them in a box.

Bill kissed Emma and then picked up the box. Emma accompanied him as he headed out the front door to take the food to the church.

"I don't know if I can bear to see those poor people again," Emma said.

"You can stay here. I'll deliver the food and come back to get you," Bill said.

"I guess I need to swallow my fear. I need to do this with you."

"Are you sure?"

"Yes. I'll go in with you." Emma really didn't want to do it, but she knew she needed to help in any way she could. The days of hiding her face in her hands were coming to a close. She had a new resolve to face the facts and the human suffering that were all around her. She was determined to take her place by her husband's side and fight the unacceptable.

Washington, DC, July 29, 1943, 1900 Local Time

Jim and Ed entered the War Room at the Pentagon after a day of tedious work on last-minute details for the operation. The room was abuzz with people on phones and others talking among themselves while examining maps and papers.

"It looks like we're well underway," Ed said.

"Yes. We may as well brace for the questioning over this operation," Jim said.

"You've obviously never met with Prime Minister Churchill," Ed said jokingly.

"I can only imagine what that's like."

"You don't know the half of it!"

The gavel banged and there was an immediate quiet around the room. The ones on the phones put them down, and everyone turned their attention to the chairman.

"I'd like to get to sleep at a godly hour tonight, so what is our reason for being here?" asked the chairman.

"Operation Saint-Nazaire," declared the clerk in his usual official voice.

"Ah, yes. Mr. Mason and Director Davies. I should have guessed."

There was the usual rumble of laughter about the room, which quickly subsided.

"You have an update for us, gentlemen?"

Ed held his hand toward Jim, indicating that Jim would speak. Jim stood up and cleared his throat.

"This is what we consider a major update on the operation. According to Adelbert Spangler, ten of the napalm drums have been moved to the east dock. This won't interfere with the original plans to facilitate a proper explosive value." He offered a pack of papers to the intern who delivered them to the chairman. "Josef Kramer is due to return to the docks tomorrow night. He's been in Berlin pitching his idea to use napalm to exterminate a great number of Jews. He's already experimented on two Jews. This act was witnessed by Lieutenant Henry Jenkins."

There was a chorus of gasps from the many people in the room. Jim paused to allow the din to subside.

"We do have a problem that wasn't considered in the plans," Jim added.

Jim leafed over to another page. "We will probably have a problem in extracting the commandos. After the degree of detonations that we've planned, there will be German ships all over the situation. If we order Allied ships to be on standby, it will tip off the Nazis that we've planned something."

Jim paused once more. General Hinckley had a wrinkled look to his face.

"Do you have a comment, General?" asked Jim.

The general leaned forward and put his elbows on the desk.

"Don't we have a way to get them out from the north? They came in that way. Can't they go back out that way?"

"The Nazi patrols will be thick. They'll have a call for all hands on deck, so to speak. The north, and all surrounding areas for that matter, will be thick with troops headed toward the docks," Jim said to General Hinckley.

"Can't Spangler help us with this?"

"He's informed us that after Kramer returns, he won't live to see the light of the next day after an incident he had with rescuing some Jews."

The general was truly angry at this point, and the veins on his neck had protruded. He thumped the desk with fist and yelled, "So you're telling me that you've put fifty of our finest troops in harm's way with no way out?"

"That's not what I'm telling you, sir" replied Jim in a calm tone. "We do have another option."

"This had better be a good option, Jim," replied a calmer general.

"I think you'll like this one, sir. We all know about the explosives rigged in the bomber. After the commandos set the explosives on the docks, they will exit and move to the north. They'll set the timer on the bomber and continue north to Saint-Malo-de-Guersac. They'll be halfway to the city before the explosions occur. We'll give them civilian clothing, and they'll blend with the locals. We can extract them later."

The general sat back and thought for a moment. "Sounds a little shaky to me."

"General, do you remember a conversation we had a few weeks ago?" The general nodded. "I remember that conversation well, Jim."

"I would hope that I could pose the same advice to you, sir. I mean no disrespect by saying that," Jim said as he bowed his head.

"I hope that this works—for both of our sakes, Jim."

Jim looked down at Ed who was giving him a thumbs-up below the level of the table. Ed smiled and nodded.

"One further update, gentlemen. We've been informed that Spangler has liberated twelve Jewish men and women who were scheduled for execution by flamethrower at the hands of Kramer. William C. McLaughton, the downed waist gunner, was responsible for getting them to safety."

There was a round of applause in the room.

Saint-Malo-de-Guersac

The Jewish people had been freed from the Nazis. They had been fed and clothed, and they were showered. They had been examined by Rabiah and had been found to be in shoddy shape, but they would eventually make full recoveries. It would just take some time.

The situation was far from perfect, but with the efforts of the good townsfolk, the Jewish people would have a much better life. Of course, any life would be better than to be starved, incinerated in the ovens, or tortured with a flamethrower.

A group had taken a seat at the big dining room table and was enjoying the time to rest and have a cup of coffee. Alexandre, Josephine, Abraham, Jeanne, Father Ambroise, Bill, and Emma sat in exhausted silence for a moment. Everyone was satisfied, at least in their own way, about the outcome of the night. They had played a part in saving people who were in desperate need of help, and it was very satisfying.

"Good job, everyone. Especially you, Bill," Alexandre said.

"I take no credit for this, Father," Bill said as he bowed his head.

Alexandre smiled at Bill and his humble spirit. Emma took Bill's hand and held it tightly.

"You're a hero," she whispered.

"Heroes are dead," Bill whispered back. The whispering wasn't necessary as everyone had heard what they had said.

Bill remembered what Henry had told him about the XO and how he had shown heroism in a time when he could have ordered someone else to take over the gun. Bill had questioned Henry about it and insisted that Henry had done the same thing as the XO—with the exception of dying, of course. Henry just shook his head and said, "Heroes are dead. Without death, a full sacrifice has not been made." Henry had insisted that he was not a hero. Bill really had no choice but to agree with the reasoning.

The group at the table began to disband. Alexandre said his good nights and helped Abraham to bed. Jeanne followed behind. Father Ambroise finished his coffee, hugged Josephine, and then made his exit. Josephine hugged Bill and Emma and made her way to bed.

"You know I have to go back to the plane," Bill said as he took Emma into his arms.

"Stay with me for a while."

"I can't. I don't mean to make you angry, but I have to go."

Emma really didn't understand the whole concept of Bill being with the troops instead of being with her, but the "new" her was willing to make sacrifices.

"Go, my love. I hope to see you again soon."

Bill kissed Emma and made his exit. There were no tears from Emma this time. She had finally adapted to be the wife of someone she considered to be a true hero.

Saint-Nazaire, July 30, 1943, 0245 Local Time

Henry breathed a sigh of relief when he got the message from Jim that Bill had gotten the Jews to safety. Bill had violated a direct order, but what was Henry going to do about it? Besides, Bill was technically MIA, and over time, had been relisted as KIA. It would be hard to explain having to discipline a dead man. He would just be glad to see his old friend again and listen to his explanation for his insubordination. For now, it was time for sleep.

Spangler fumbled under his desk for the Enigma machine. He set it on his desk, unclipped the radio that Bill had given him, and laid it on the desk beside the machine. He thought of his treason against the Third Reich. The actions that he had taken to destroy the operations at Saint-Nazaire were justified in his own mind, but he knew there would be consequences from the regime. Most undoubtedly, his death.

He was prepared for the consequences. He had no regrets. He was ready for the confrontation with Kramer that was sure to take place as soon as he returned from Berlin.

Kramer removed the Luger pistol from the bottom drawer of his desk and laid it beside the machine and the radio. The Luger was a 1938 Walther P38, and the magazine was capable of firing 9 mm rounds. The magazine held eight rounds in total. He was sure that he only needed one.

Bill arrived back at camp and entered the plane. Henry was sound asleep on the bags in the tail of the bomber. Bill was exhausted from all the activity, so he climbed on the bags and fell into a deep sleep almost immediately. He had certainly earned his rest.

In the midst of his sleep, the nightmare began again. It had always been the same in the past, with a few extras added for good measure. Bill tossed lightly and grimaced. He heard the words "well played" echoing in his head. The words "lead the target" echoed as a whisper over and over again. There was a blinding explosion, and an intense flame leaped forward from the shadows. Then the fiery image appeared as it always did.

Bill had become accustomed to waking in a sitting position, and this was just another day, another nightmare. His eyes opened, but his vision was not functioning quite properly yet. He felt a hand on his shoulder.

"Bill! Bill!"

The voice was distant. His vision was finally working, and he saw Henry in front of him and felt his gentle shakes. Bill was drenched in sweat, and he was breathing rapidly.

"Are you okay, buddy?" Henry asked with concern in his voice.

"Yeah. I'm okay," Bill said.

"You're having a lot of nightmares lately."

"I know. I know."

Bill was not okay. He remembered what Alexandre had told him about dreams while he was convalescing in his bed. Could this be an omen of things to come? What did it mean? He was always left with more questions and no answers.

"You did a good job on that rescue," Henry said with a frown.

"Well, thank you, sir. Why the frown?"

"But you disobeyed a direct order for reconnaissance only."

"I was interrupted by Spangler. I had no choice but to do what I did."

"Yeah. I heard from Jim Mason."

"I gave Spangler my radio."

Henry frowned at the idea of a Nazi having one of their radios, but under the circumstances, Spangler was a trusted ally to their cause. "I'll get you another radio. And I guess we need to talk about tonight."

Saint-Malo-de-Guersac

Daylight had broken, and Emma had not slept at all. She stayed in her bed and looked up at the ceiling with her thoughts running rampant. She swiveled sideways on the bed and began to get dressed. She tied her shoes and then went to the mirror, only to be frightened by her own reflection.

The lack of sleep was beginning to take a toll on her. The worry and stress of having a husband who was determined to destroy all the evil in the world was more than enough to cause the bags beneath her eyes. She was an old woman at the tender age of nineteen.

Emma stepped through the back door of the house and into the dining room. Father and Mother were both seated in their usual places drinking coffee.

"Good morning, dear. You should be resting," her father said.

"I tried and failed," Emma said. "I'm too concerned to rest."

Josephine understood all too well what Emma was feeling. She, too, had had those sleepless nights of concern when Alexandre had traveled on business or had been away taking care of other issues.

After the conversation Alexandre and Emma had about her need to visit the plane, Alexandre was afraid that she would venture out on her own. He was hoping that common sense would take precedence over her desperate need to make sure that her husband was safe. Common sense rarely trumped desperation, and Alexandre knew it.

"Sit with us and have some coffee, dear," Alexandre said.

Emma sat, and her mother went to the kitchen to get her a cup of coffee. Alexandre looked at Emma. "So, what are your plans for the day, dear?"

"I want to go to the church to see if I can lend a hand."

"That's a good goal, dear. How do you hope to help?"

Emma thought on the question for a moment. It was actually a good question, and she was unsure about how to answer it.

"I'll just ask Father Ambroise for guidance. He'll know what needs to be done. I'll probably take some food with me."

Alexandre was pleased with the answer she had given. He was also pleased that he had used reverse psychology to get his point across—in her complete oblivion. By making her think of the Jews in the church, he had given her a cause that would hopefully keep her mind busy and off the possibility that she would feel the need to go help Bill.

Josephine returned with an extra cup and the coffeepot. She poured the cups full for all at the table, and then they sat in silence for several minutes. Each was thinking of the stress that had been placed on their emotional and psychological plates.

CHAPTER 20

Saint-Nazaire, July 30, 1943, 0700 Local Time

All fifty of the commandos had arrived, and Henry was busy with the briefing of the raid that was to occur at midnight. He had assigned the teams of ten and given assignments to the teams.

Bill had not been assigned to a team. Since he would be the odd man out, he would operate the waist gun when the time came.

After the briefing, the teams went to have breakfast and discuss their assignments.

Henry stepped back in the plane. Bill was checking the charges that had been attached to the six thousand pounds of high-explosive bombs in the bomb bay. The bombs had been accessorized with twenty pounds of RDX plastics, which had enough force to decimate two square miles in a very short period of time. The bombs would act as an incendiary that would roll out a flame of epic proportions, destroying anything in its path. Sand would be turned into glass.

"You know we'll have to manually activate these bombs, right?" Bill said as he looked at the pinwheel-activation fans.

"Yeah. I know. We can activate them after we set the timer on the plastics."

The bombs were equipped with safety devices so they couldn't be detonated as they were being loaded or before they left the bomb bay. As they were dropped from the bays, the pinwheels on the sides would be stimulated by the outside air. They would spin and deactivate the safety devices.

Henry said, "This is going to be a tight operation. One slight screwup— and we'll lose the whole shooting match."

There was a crackle on Henry's two-way radio.

Bill and Henry stopped talking and listened to the crackling. There was definitely a voice, but what was being said was a complete mystery.

The voice became clearer.

"Bill? Are you there, Bill?"

Henry detached the radio from his belt and handed it to Bill.

"Yes? This is Bill."

"This is Adelbert. I need to speak with you."

"In private? I can meet you somewhere."

"Can you meet me at the church? I can rearrange the guard so you can get free passage."

"Of course. I'll be there."

"I'll meet you in an hour?"

"I'll be there."

Henry looked at Bill. "Any idea what this is about?"

"Not a clue. We'll find out soon enough."

"You know you have to do this by yourself. I can't risk being seen."

"It'll be okay, brother. Everything will be just fine."

"You'd better get going. You don't want to be late."

Saint-Malo-de-Guersac

Emma had made it to the church with her tray of food. It was a beautiful old church made almost entirely of stone. It reminded her of the church back in Saint-Nazaire, minus the steeple and the fact that this church wasn't in ruins. Sadly, it didn't have a place to use for a perch.

She had stopped looking at the steeple and looked back at where she was walking and had to stop in her tracks. There stood Father Ambroise right in front of her. She had nearly collided with him.

"Hello, Emma," Father Ambroise said with a smile.

"I'm sorry, Father Ambroise. I guess I need to watch where I'm walking."

"It's okay, dear. Lots of people admire the church and forget that they're walking."

Emma giggled. She'd always liked Father Ambroise. He was a kind man, and he always had nice words for anyone he met. "I've got a tray of food for the Jewish people. I'd like to deliver it personally, if possible."

"Of course, dear. Right this way."

Emma had always loved the floral smell of church. It reminded her of being in a field with a clear blue sky above her. She enjoyed the echo of her footsteps as she walked down the marble aisle between the pews. The red and blue glow of light from the sun shining through the stained glass windows made the church lively and friendly. It was a peaceful place, and she'd have to make it a point to go there more often, if for nothing more than just to sit and enjoy the peaceful atmosphere.

At the front of the sanctuary, Father Ambroise opened the door leading to the classrooms. He held the door for Emma, and she smiled and nodded as she entered the hallway. She had not been nervous up to that point, but she realized that she was going to have to face people who had experienced pure evil. She would have to wear a smile—even if it was fake. The Jews had earned a chance at happiness, and Emma was determined to do everything in her power to make sure they were happy.

Emma paused before entering the room. She drew in a deep breath and put on the most cheerful smile that she could muster.

Father Ambroise said, "You don't have to do this. You can hand me the tray, and I'll do it for you." He pulled the door shut to give Emma a chance to discuss her fears.

Emma looked at Father Ambroise with sadness. "Bless me, Father, for I have sinned," Emma said with a tear in her eye.

Father Ambroise kissed the cross that was dangling from his neck. He took the tray from Emma and opened the door to the room containing the Jewish people. "Sister Avery, will you take this tray to the kitchen?" Father Ambroise then closed the door, took Emma by the hand, and led her to the confessional.

Emma sat on the bench, and the window slid open.

Father Ambroise said, "I can see by the tears in your eyes that you are truly contrite."

"I am, Father." Emma crossed her chest with the symbol of the cross. "In the name of the Father, and the Son, and the Holy Spirit. This is my first confession. I have never been in a confessional."

"Say the sins that you remember, my child," Father Ambroise said.

"My sin is selfishness. I wasn't even aware that I was being selfish." Emma paused to allow the wave of sorrow to pass. Her voice had become squeaky at the end of her statement, and she didn't want to sob during the confession.

"Take your time, my child. We're in no rush here."

Emma dabbed at the tears with the collar on her shirt. "I have claimed my husband as mine and mine alone. I have sinned against God and my mother. I told my mother, in so many words, that I would do as I please. My love for my husband blinded me."

Father Ambroise knew exactly what Emma was talking about. He offered some advice.

"Go to your mother and express your contrition to her. Hug her. Kiss her on the cheek. Let her know that she is a good source for advice."

"Yes, Father. I'll do that."

Emma prayed the Act of Contrition, exited the confessional, and went back to the room where the Jews were located.

Father Ambroise opened the door and Emma entered. She was smiling, and this time the smile was not forced. She was happy to be able to help.

Alexandre was in his usual place, working the fields. He was happy with his place in life and knew that his efforts were feeding his family and the Brodeurs whom he now he considered part of his family.

Alexandre heard the sound of traffic on the road that ran along the boundary of the field. It was a Nazi convoy. This time, it was a big one. As it got closer, he could see that there was a truck that had gun turrets on it. The next two trucks were prison trucks. There were two other trucks behind that—and then two more prison trucks. The last truck had the same gun turrets attached to it as the first one.

After the trucks passed, Alexandre knelt in the field. He had no idea why he had knelt or what he was praying for. It was a reflex, but he felt that he needed to kneel. An ominous feeling had come over him. He prayed for Emma. He prayed that God would give her strength. It was as if an inspiration had passed over him, and he just prayed.

When the prayer was finished, Alexandre rose. A tear was streaming down his cheek, and this puzzled him. He wiped the tear away and continued with his work.

Saint-Nazaire

Bill made it to the church and walked around to the front of the ruins. He had no idea where Spangler would be since they had not determined an exact meeting place, and he decided to stand inside the walls.

"Bill? I'm up here," Spangler said.

Bill looked up and saw Spangler on the perch.

"Come and join me. There's a spectacular view from up here."

Bill climbed the crude stairs and stood next to Spangler.

Spangler said, "I never realized how beautiful the world could be from a vantage point such as this."

"It is spectacular, Adelbert. My wife used this place for thought. She referred to it as her perch," Bill said with a smile.

"I had a reason for needing to have this conversation in private, Bill. I needed to bring you certain information that you and your allies refer to as *intel*."

"I'm all ears," Bill said as he folded his arms across his chest. This was a gesture that was very familiar to Spangler, and he smiled at the prospect that Bill might have caught the habit by proximity.

Spangler drew in a breath. "General Major Josef Kramer will return this evening. There are events that will unfold as a result." Spangler instinctively folded his arms across his chest, not as a mocking, but rather as a force of habit.

"You need to be careful with your movements. Kramer is a very smart man, and he will be able to see what is happening if any of your people are spotted. I won't be able to do anything else to help you and your commandos after his return. I will, most likely, be dead."

Bill looked down at the floor of the perch as he thought about the prospect of Spangler's death. He had become a friend for the operation and a personal friend for Bill. The thought of him dying for the sake of the success of the operation was cause for Bill to never doubt the sincerity of this unlikely ally. "You don't have to die, Adelbert."

"I don't expect for you to understand my moral dilemma, Bill. I am obliged to see this operation through to the last minute of my life. Things that need to be attended to will be attended to."

"You are indeed a good man, Adelbert. It will be sad to lose you as a friend," Bill said. "I wish I could do something to help you."

"There's really nothing that anyone can say to change my mind. I will not run from what I have helped set in motion. I don't even expect you to understand that," Spangler said.

Bill really didn't understand, but he decided to remain objective. He had developed the deepest of respect for Spangler, and everyone involved in the operation should be grateful that they had his invaluable help. And now, this man was willing to sacrifice his life to ensure the destruction of what he knew was wrong.

"There's one other thing. There are twelve Jews due to arrive here at any time. There's nothing I can do to save them," Spangler said as he hung his head.

"Well, that's certainly not good. I'll have to see if we can do something about that."

Bill had no idea what he could possibly do. The rescue of the previous twelve people had been difficult enough, and he had had Spangler's help. Now there were an additional twelve?

"We'll have to see what we can do for them after the operation. I really don't know how we're going to help them at all," Bill said.

"You've proven to me that you are resilient. You've survived a plane crash and serious injuries. You've rescued people from sure death at the risk of your own life. I'm sure you'll figure something out," Spangler said, patting Bill on the shoulder.

He extended his hand to Bill, and Bill grasped it in a tight grip.

"You're a true soldier, Bill. It has been my honor and my privilege to deal with you."

"The honor is all mine, Adelbert. I just wish we'd have met under different circumstances."

Spangler and Bill went their separate ways. Both men had regrets of things they hadn't said to the other.

Dieter Schmidt was standing on the west dock in guard of the prisoners as he waited for his relief to take over. His relief was Klaus Fischer, and they were friends from way back in school.

"Good afternoon, Dieter!" came a familiar voice.

"Klaus," said Dieter. "So glad you could be here."

Dieter looked back and forth between Klaus and his watch. Both men laughed as if it were truly comical. They saluted each other as was the custom for Nazi soldiers whenever a guard was changed. The two men stepped into the guard shack and looked both ways as they entered.

Klaus said, "Do you plan to talk to Lieutenant Spangler?"

"Yes—but I don't know how approachable he'll be."

"This has to be done. If you'd like, I'll do it."

Dieter said, "No. I'll talk to him. I hope he's the man Jim Mason says he is. Otherwise, he'll kill me on the spot."

"You are a brave man, Dieter. I've always respected you."

Dieter stepped out of the guard shack and made his way to do his deed.

Bill entered the bomber with a worried look on his face. Henry looked up and immediately surmised that Bill had gotten news that was not so favorable.

"You look worried, old friend," Henry said. Bill and Henry were relatively new friends, but Henry used the word "old" as a term of endearment.

"Not so much worried—just concerned," replied Bill.

"Care to share your concern?"

"There are twelve more Jews at the west dock."

Henry sighed deeply. Here was that moral dilemma again.

"You know the operation is tonight, right?"

Bill nodded. He was painfully aware of his inability to help these people in need, and it caused him great sorrow.

"We'll have to sit this one out, brother," Henry said, referring to the rescuing of the Jews.

Bill nodded again. "That's what bothers me. This will be on my conscience forever." Bill knew that being a military man was not going to be an easy job when he signed up for it, but he had not realized that nonbattle decisions would be this difficult. Sometimes he wished that he was a battle-hardened soldier without all the guilt attached to it.

Dieter walked up the stairs to the lieutenant's office and stood there for a moment. He wasn't looking forward to this conversation. He just hoped that his intel was correct—and that the lieutenant was on board with the plans. Dieter knocked on the door.

"Yes?" came a voice from inside.

Dieter opened the door and walked into the lieutenant's office.

"What is it?" growled the lieutenant.

"I need to speak with you on an urgent matter, sir."

"Well? Speak up!"

"Jim … Mason."

Spangler's jaw immediately dropped, and he was at a loss for words.

"I was hoping we could have a conversation, sir," said Dieter.

Spangler stood up and walked to the big picture window. He folded his arms across his chest, then he turned to face Dieter.

Spangler said, "What is it that you need from me?"

"We infiltrated your efforts here at the docks two months ago."

"Who is *we*?"

"Forgive me, sir. Klaus Fischer is my partner."

Spangler was very confused.

"Infiltrated? Partner?"

"Yes, sir. We are OSS agents, and we were sent by Agent Mason to watch you. I know this sounds like distrust, but you have to admit, sir, that war is a distrustful and distasteful human function."

Spangler understood this sentiment. Being a Nazi was cause for the Allies to question his integrity. It didn't anger him that Jim had watched him. It was actually a relief to know that he now had two others to help him in this godforsaken place. Spangler softened his attitude in light of the information that Dieter had just shared with him.

"What is it that you need from me?" Spangler said.

"We've been in constant contact with Agent Mason. He's telling us that we need to free the Jewish prisoners. He wants them to be taken to the church in Saint-Malo-de-Guersac."

"That was a major concern of mine," Spangler said with a sigh of relief.

"If you can clear the guard on the outer perimeter, Klaus and I will usher the good people out of here."

"I'll be glad to do that," Spangler said. "I just have one question."

"And what would that be, sir?"

"Why didn't Jim tell me this himself?"

"We couldn't risk someone intercepting the message. Your name was never mentioned in our communications. It was easier and more secure this way."

Spangler understood. He would have done the same thing if the roles were reversed.

"I sometimes wish I had been born in one of the Allied countries," Spangler said. "Being a Nazi is part of my heritage, but it is not part of my moral fiber."

Saint-Malo-de-Guersac

Emma had gotten dressed. It felt good to have a few hours of sleep. She was geared and ready for the day. She and her mother, along with Jeanne, sat at the kitchen table drinking coffee.

Josephine said, "What's on your agenda today?"

"I'm going to the church to help out."

Josephine had had several moments when she was proud of Emma in the past few weeks, and this was definitely one of those moments.

"I'll help you make a tray of food," Jeanne said.

"Thank you, Mrs. Brodeur," Emma said with a smile.

Jeanne was happy to have the Bellerose family in her home, and she was glad to see Emma happy. The first few days had been a hurdle for Emma; she had been despondent, so Jeanne was relieved when she had perked up. Emma missed Bill, but no one had brought up the subject for obvious reasons. Part of the healing process included being able to grieve in silence.

To Emma, it was a pleasure preparing food to take to the church, and she smiled whenever she served the Jewish people. These people had survived things that were nightmarish to say the least, and it scared Emma to think the Nazis would not even hesitate to put her and her family through the same treatment.

Emma and Jeanne finished making food for the church, and Emma put a clean towel over the tray. She said her goodbyes and headed out the front door.

She arrived at the church and climbed the steps, and as usual, she admired the architecture. She was always in awe at the beauty of this place. The Jews had been taken out of a bad place and been put in a good place. This thought made her smile.

Saint-Nazaire

Henry was peering through the waist gun window and through the space between the trees at the roadway that ran between the west dock and the guard shack.

"Looking at anything in particular?" said Bill.

"Yeah. Look at this." Bill took the binoculars and saw a prison truck on its way out of the west dock.

"What do you make of that?" asked Henry.

"It looks like they did the same thing I did. They loaded all the prisoners on one truck."

"That's a little odd in my book. I wish I knew what was happening," Henry said, shrugging his shoulders.

And just like that, the radio crackled to life.

"Bill?" came a voice from the radio.

Henry handed the radio to Bill with a deeply surprised look on his face.

"Adelbert?"

"I need to make this quick. The Jewish people are on their way to safety. No time to explain."

"Yes. I was wondering about that."

"Take care, Bill. Good luck on the operation."

Bill handed the radio back to Henry.

"This is very odd!" Henry said. "We need to figure out what's going on. We don't need any wrinkles in this operation. Are the rescuers Nazis? That doesn't make a bit of sense."

Saint-Malo-de-Guersac, July 30, 1943, 1105 Local Time

Emma was enjoying the opportunity to feed the Jewish people in the church, and they were responsive to her kindness. She hadn't been so happy in a long time. If she couldn't be with her husband, then this was the next best thing. The time for psychological healing was well on its way. Father Ambroise was standing next to her in guidance of her care for the Jewish people.

The door to the dining room opened, and Sister Avery walked in. She came over to Father Ambroise and said in a soft voice,

"You're needed at the back door, Father. More Jews coming in."

Father Ambroise said, "Come with me, Emma. I may need you."

They made their way to the door where two Nazi soldiers stood. They removed their hats and smiled as Father Ambroise and the two ladies appeared. This behavior was highly unusual for Nazi soldiers. They were usually not friendly, and they were certainly not so gracious as to show respect for anyone who was not German.

Dieter said, "We're not Nazis. I'm Dieter, and this is my partner, Klaus."

Klaus nodded.

"We have twelve Jews who need protection." Dieter motioned to the truck.

Father Ambroise and Emma looked in, and it was the same sight they had seen before. Emma covered her mouth, but she was beyond tears at this point. Her main concern was getting these poor people clothed and fed. Her dislike for the Nazis had grown deeper after seeing the people they had tortured and abused, and it made her all the more determined to help.

The five of them got the Jews inside and down to the dining room. Sister Avery went to gather some clothes, and Father Ambroise and Emma went into the kitchen to round up some food.

Father Ambroise said, "So, where do you go from here?"

Dieter said, "We're heading back to Saint-Nazaire. We have business to attend to there." The sight of the Jews got the wheels turning in Emma's mind. Her husband was in danger. She had made a pact with herself that she would not interfere—due partly to the fact that she was unqualified to offer assistance and also because she didn't want her parents to worry—but she wanted to be with Bill. It was a moral dilemma, and yet she wanted to somehow get justice for the mistreatment of not only her home town but also to the people she was now helping.

Dieter and Klaus got back into the prison truck and headed out.

Father Ambroise looked at Emma. "You look worried, dear."

"I'm okay. I need to get inside and help these people."

Father Ambroise was satisfied that all was good with Emma.

Washington, DC, July 30, 1943, 0630 Local Time

Jim and Ed had made it an early day as they stepped into Jim's office at the Pentagon. Jim was a bundle of nerves, and Ed knew it.

"Relax, Jim. This may go better than you expect," Ed said.

"I know. It's the same old thoughts over and over again. People are going to die today, and I had a hand in making the deaths a reality."

"Not to beat a dead horse, but always remember that more people would have died had it not been for this operation."

Jim nodded. "I guess we need to get down to the War Room. They'll have maps set up with real-time movements."

"Are you ready for this?" Ed shot a sideways glance at Jim.

"As ready as I'll ever be," Jim said.

The War Room was full of people in military uniforms. There were the usual nods and handshakes as the two friends made their way to their seats. The maps along the wall were lit, and the movements of all military vessels were clearly visible.

"It looks like we've got German ships headed toward ground zero," Ed said. "Do you know why I'm the director of MI6?"

"I don't know, Ed. I guess I never thought about it."

"I was involved in an operation in Germany. I didn't want to do it, but I knew it was one of the reasons I had signed up for the spy game. It was not up to me to pick and choose what I was supposed to do."

Jim said, "I remember the glamourous thoughts I had when I joined the OSS. Those thoughts were dashed when I found out that it was no picnic."

"Exactly! I was sent to Berlin as a spy. I had to send information back to MI6, and I had to kill people in the process. Even though they were bad people, I still had nightmares. It's okay to have thoughts of remorse. Those thoughts will pass. Sure, you'll have nightmares. When they occur, just sit up on the bed and think about all the lives that were saved because of your actions. Peace comes with a price."

Jim nodded.

"Now, about those ships," Ed said. "Looks like two German battleships and a destroyer are headed to the docks."

"I have no idea how that translates," Jim said.

"I've got a little experience in this respect. See the red marks on the blips that represent the ships?"

Jim nodded.

Ed said, "Those are damaged ships. The varying degrees of red show how badly they're damaged. These damages were estimated by the Allied ships that damaged them. We need to get in touch with Spangler to get more information on those ships."

"I'll go get the machine."

Saint-Nazaire

Henry watched the prison truck as it rolled back toward the west dock. There were no faces peering through the windows and no hands gripping the bars.

Bill entered the plane and said, "What do you see, boss?"

Henry didn't take his eyes off the truck. "It's apparently an empty prison truck. The same truck we saw earlier."

"We have to believe that Adelbert got the prisoners to safety. I hope they are at the church in Saint-Malo-de-Guersac," Bill said. "Father Ambroise will take good care of them!"

"Are you ready for tonight, Bill?" Henry put down his binoculars.

"I s'pose. It's going to be a hard fight. We probably need to catch some rest in shifts."

Henry nodded. "You go ahead and catch some shut-eye. I'll keep watch from here."

Bill climbed on the few sacks that were left in the back of the plane. Most of the sacks contained boxes of grenades that needed to be distributed among the commandos before the operation.

Spangler removed his Enigma machine from the hiding place and turned it on. A message started to scribe itself onto the rolled paper: "Three ships headed to you. How badly are they damaged?" A second message came through as well: "We need to use those ships as weapons. You need to get out of there."

Adelbert composed a message back to Jim: "Ships are heavily damaged with little use of weapons. I'll be fine. Take care of your own, my friend."

Spangler put the machine back in its hiding place, picked up the radio, and switched it on. "This is Adelbert."

Henry reached down for his radio. "This is Henry."

"The Jews are safe at the church in Saint-Malo-de-Guersac."

"That's good news."

"This is the last time we can talk. Good luck tonight."

"Good luck to you, Adelbert." Henry put the radio back on his belt and shook his head.

Saint-Malo-de-Guersac

In the Brodeur home, it was time for coffee and discussing the events of the day.

Alexandre said, "Well, this is the big night, I suppose."

"I guess my major concern is for the safety of this family," Abraham said. "We're a little close to the action for my comfort."

Jeanne smiled.

"We need to stay put," Josephine said. "We've run far enough. We've survived adversity—and we'll survive again."

The men glanced at one another.

"I think you're right, dear," Alexandre said with a smile. "If we try to move away, we'll probably be going into more danger."

Abraham took another sip of coffee. "Then it's settled. We stay."

Emma cleared her throat.

Alexandre said, "Something on your mind, dear?"

"It was a personal thought, and now the thought has passed."

"There's no judgment here. Speak your mind, dear."

Emma drew in a breath and looked at the table. "I'd like to be at the church when the action starts. I want to help take care of the Jewish people. I was going to suggest that we all go. It's got to be the safest place in the city."

Josephine took Emma by the hand as a tear rolled down her face.

Alexandre smiled. "You go take care of them, dear. We'll be fine here."

"I don't want to seem like I'm abandoning you," Emma said.

Alexandre said, "You've taken on the responsibility of caring for the Jewish people, dear. That is very commendable. We'll be fine."

CHAPTER 21

Saint-Nazaire

Bill woke up in his usual upright position, sweating and disoriented.

"Same old nightmare?" Henry said.

"Yes. With more previews this time."

"Wanna talk about it?"

"Everything is the same except for a new player. Can I see that picture in your pocket?"

Henry reached in his coat pocket and handed Bill the picture of Van Landingham.

"That's the same guy. He's in the nightmare. He's dressed in his best navy blues."

"Are you sure about that? Maybe seeing the picture was just the power of suggestion. Did it trigger something in your mind?" Henry tapped the picture with his finger. "After all, this man is dead."

"I'm absolutely sure it was him. He saluted me and said something to me that I couldn't fully understand."

"Oh?"

"He said that the target was stationary, so there was no point in leading it. I'm paraphrasing. He said it differently, I just can't remember exactly what he said. He appeared out of a fog, or some sort of a smoke screen. After he spoke, the fog or smoke or whatever engulfed him, and he disappeared."

"That's really strange, my friend. Are you okay now?"

"Yeah. I'm okay. You need to get some sleep, Henry."

"Time for sleep has come and gone. I've got a show to run here."

Bill nodded. He was sorry that he had slept for so long. Henry could have used some of that time to rest. Bill felt badly that he had been so selfish.

"Are you okay for the operation?" Henry said.

"I wouldn't miss it for the world, brother."

"Good. We can use a good gunner. Firing that waist gun should be 'old hat' for you," Henry said with a wry grin.

"You've got more experience as a gunner than I do," Bill said.

"I s'pose, but that turret gun was different than freezing to death at an open window."

"I'll still be by the open window, but at least I won't be freezing to death."

They laughed. It was a nervous sort of laughter since both men knew the night would be extremely perilous.

"You wanted to see me, sir?" asked Dieter.

Spangler looked up from the paperwork on his desk. "Yes. I have a mission for you and Klaus."

"Yes, sir?"

"You two don't belong here. When I say that, I mean that you don't need to have to die tonight."

"Our mission is complete, sir. We thought you might need a little more help."

"All the wheels are in motion. There's nothing left to do. I need you to get out of here before the general major returns. After that, you'll be trapped."

Dieter wrinkled his face. He was pained by the thought of Spangler facing the demon alone. "You mentioned a mission, sir?"

"I need you to deliver a message to the church in Saint-Malo-de-Guersac."

"A message, sir?"

"Yes. I need you to tell the minister that there may be repercussions from the operation tonight. If the general major survives, he may go after the surrounding towns. I don't know how many of the commandos will survive, but I'm sure it won't be enough to protect the Jewish people in the church. There is an outside chance that they'll be in danger, but we need to get the word out to cover all our bases."

"Consider it done, sir." Dieter exited the office.

Spangler took out his Enigma machine and the Allied radio. "This is Adelbert."

There was a pause. Spangler certainly hoped that he would be able to talk to Henry or Bill. He had told them that they wouldn't hear from him again, but this was important.

"This is Henry."

"Henry, two soldiers will be passing your position in a few minutes. Let them pass. They are friendly."

"Will do."

Spangler put down his radio and fired up the Enigma for one last message to Jim. It had been a long journey to get to where he was. He was a friend to goodness and purity. He was a friend to the downtrodden. He was both a friend and an ally to the people who were going to crush the Nazi dream of building weapons and vessels of destruction. Spangler was prepared to face his fate with no regrets.

Saint-Malo-de-Guersac

Emma had arrived at the church with the usual admiration of the architecture. She once again stood in amazement at the steeple and reminisced about the times she had spent on her perch in Saint-Nazaire. She remembered the bad thoughts and the good ones. She remembered Bill holding her as they looked at the stars and enjoyed each other's company. Emma entered the church doors and made her way to the dining hall. She had a mixture of emotions. She was happy to be helping people, yet she was apprehensive about the safety of her husband. She was deeply in love with Bill, and that reality brought with it an entirely different mix of emotions. She had shown restraint in not going to be with him. It would have been selfish, and it would have put him in more danger due to the added responsibility of protecting her.

As Emma came to the dining hall, she heard voices. They were coming from the minister's office. They were male voices, and Emma had not remembered there being any men in the church except for Father

Ambroise. The voices puzzled her, so she stood next to the closed door and tried to listen.

"Sent to warn you, sir," said a man.

Emma had joined the conversation late. She was hoping that she could hear enough of the rest of the conversation to figure out what the warning was about.

"I don't know what else I can do. There's really no other place to hide the Jewish people."

"We'll do what we can to help," a different voice replied.

Father Ambroise sighed heavily. "I never thought I'd hear myself say this, but let's just hope that the general major dies tonight. God forgive me for saying that."

"You're not in need of forgiveness, sir. You are protecting twenty-four innocent souls from one evil soul—if he even has a soul. Your wish for his death is warranted in this situation," said a soft and consoling voice.

Emma was sobbing softly when she heard footsteps in the hallway. She looked up and it was Sister Avery.

"Are you alright, Emma?" said Sister Avery as she reached into her pocket and handed Emma a tissue.

Emma put her finger to her lips and motioned down the hall.

The two women walked a few feet and stopped to talk.

"Please tell Father Ambroise that I'm not feeling well, and I need to go home," Emma said.

"Take care, dear. I'm here to talk if you need me."

Emma ran down the hall to the back door and disappeared into the darkness.

Father Ambroise emerged from the office with Dieter and Klaus. Father Ambroise could see the distressed look on Sister Avery's face.

"What's troubling you, Sister?

"It's Emma. She said that she's not feeling well and needed to go home."

Father Ambroise wrinkled his brow. He remembered the talk he had had with Emma about missing Bill. He looked at Dieter and Klaus.

"I need you to go back and keep Emma safe. She's headed back to Saint-Nazaire."

Dieter said, "We'll do that, sir."

Sister Avery covered her mouth and gasped. "I could have stopped her."

Father Ambroise said, "You couldn't have stood in the way of love, Sister. You did fine."

Alexandre, Josephine, and the Brodeurs were enjoying their evening coffee when they heard a loud squeak.

"Whatever could that have been?" asked Josephine as she shot a glance toward the back door of the house.

Alexandre didn't even look. He knew it was Emma, and he knew what she was doing. Alexandre stood up and kissed Josephine on the forehead.

"You know what I have to do," Alexandre said. "I love you. I always have and always will."

Josephine began to cry and put her face in her hands.

Emma slipped through the door of the shed and quickly retrieved the pair of binoculars that Bill had left her, and then she made haste to exit the door before anyone found her out.

Alexandre bid his goodbyes to the Brodeurs and exited the back door of the house. It was a long journey, and he was not actually able to run. He walked as quickly as he could.

Emma ran while tears streamed down her face. She was hoping that she would not be too late. Late for what? She was unsure of how she could help, but she knew she couldn't just stand by and do nothing—at least according to her own reasoning.

Saint-Nazaire

Spangler was expecting Kramer back at any time, so he had to hurry and finish the work he had started. He walked onto the west dock and gave the command to pull the two large battleships into the dry docks. This new position would maximize the damage from the initial blasts and the intense and unquenchable fireball that would emit from each installment along the submarine nets.

Spangler's radio crackled to life.

"Lieutenant?"

"Yes?"

"The general major's boat has arrived at the east dock."

"Good. Let him know that it's urgent that I see him."

Spangler put his radio back on his side and made his way to the office. As he walked, he admired the structure that had taken so many months to build—and the construction that was due to be completed over the next few months. He chuckled to himself about the fact that the construction would never be finished.

Henry made his way out to the men encamped on the left side of the bomber to group them together and get ready to move. Each commando had a radio and was equipped with a pistol and a machine gun. They had the usual decoration of hand grenades adorned about the belt and a spare chain of ammo crisscrossed around the chest and back. Each man was also equipped with a nine-inch blade strapped to a leg. The plastics and diving suits were located at the cove—along with the timing mechanisms.

Henry said, "Okay. Listen up, guys. First ten, move to the cove now. All spotters get to your appointed area."

The men began to advance toward the cove. The church offered a great deal of cover, and Spangler had planned for all patrols to be out of the area.

Kramer stepped off the boat and noticed that Spangler was not there to greet him. Instead, he had sent a soldier.

"Where is Lieutenant Spangler?" growled Kramer.

"He sent me to meet you, sir." The soldier saluted. "The lieutenant says it's urgent that you and he speak."

"Get on your radio and have the west dock guard tie the Jews to trees. I'm going to have some fun tonight."

The soldier stood there with the radio in his hand.

Kramer's veins stood out on his neck. "Didn't you hear me?"

"I heard you, sir. There are no Jewish people here."

"What? Explain!"

"Lieutenant Spangler sent them away."

Kramer was beside himself with rage. "Why would Spangler do that? You're coming with me! We're going to arrest him!"

Emma made it to the edge of the forest behind the church, crouched behind the bushes, and watched the ten commandos pass by just fifty yards in front of her. When the coast was clear, she made her move to get to the church and up to her perch.

Henry's radio crackled.

"Lieutenant?"

"Go ahead."

"There appears to be a young woman running toward the old church."

"Keep an eye on her. I think I know who it is. We can't intervene at this point."

"Will do."

Henry returned the radio to his belt and made his way back into the bomber.

Emma had made it to the church and entered the back door. The place was a mess. The Nazi soldiers had ransacked it looking for God only knew what. The place brought back memories that she never thought she'd miss. She longed for the days when she was with all the people she had known closely for the past two years.

She climbed the stairs from the crypt and went up to the perch. She sat on the bench, took the binoculars from around her neck, and placed them to her eyes. The docks were quiet. Eerily quiet. Too quiet for her comfort. She longed for Bill to be seated next to her.

Spangler was standing next to the big picture window in his office. He had his arms folded across his chest, which was the usual for him. He watched as Kramer came into the building from the docks with the soldier in tow. Kramer looked up at the window and snarled.

Spangler heard the footsteps on the stairs as Kramer stomped down on each step in anger. The door to the office opened and hit the wall. It was almost as if Kramer had kicked the door as he got to it.

Kramer screamed, "What have you done, Spangler?"

Spangler didn't answer. He just stood there.

"I asked you a question!"

Spangler sighed and turned to face Kramer. His arms remained crossed. "I'll tell you what I've done. I've turned my back on the idea that we are a master race. I've rejected the idea of killing innocent people just so you can satisfy your need to carry out your demonic way of thought. I decided I would do my part to end the oppression of the Nazis. I'm really surprised you didn't see what I was doing all along. Could it be that you're not as intelligent as you think you are?"

Kramer stepped back. He was surprised that his most-trusted lieutenant, even with their differences, had betrayed his own party. Kramer was truly angry! He stood there spitting and sputtering as he tried to comprehend what he had just heard.

The soldier raised his rifle and pointed the barrel at Spangler.

"You're under arrest, Spangler! I'll see you hang!" growled Kramer.

Spangler smiled. "You'll never get that pleasure … sir!" Spangler unfolded his arms and exposed the Luger that was in his right hand. He had tucked the pistol under his left armpit as his arms were folded. He placed the barrel of the pistol against his right temple.

"Die Tat Ist Vollbracht!" Spangler said as he smiled and pulled the trigger. He fell. Blood began to drain from the wound, down his face, and onto the floor. He was still holding the Luger. His eyes were open, and the smile never left his face.

"A quick death was too good for you … *schmutzig schwein!*"

The fourth team had made it to the cove and donned their scuba gear. The first team had returned and had begun preparations to take positions around the cove area to provide cover in case the operation was compromised.

Charges had been set all along the west dock and the submarine netting. Fifty pounds of plastic explosives were set every fifty yards. That may have seemed like overkill, but the facility at the west dock was reinforced with eight-foot-thick walls with steel girders on top of and underneath with additional girders sandwiched in between. The plastics would cause a firestorm that would kill anyone near the facility—even if the facility wasn't completely destroyed.

Henry was standing at the waist gunner's window with his arms folded across his chest.

Bill was doing his final check on the waist gun as he shot several glances over to Henry. "What's going on, Henry?"

"Huh? Oh, nothing. Just got my mind on the operation."

"I know you well enough to know that you're thinking about something else."

Henry looked at the floor. He didn't want to tell Bill that Emma was at the church, but he knew he couldn't betray his friend by withholding that sort of information. "I've got something to tell you, but you've got to promise you won't panic."

Bill was troubled by this statement, but he chose to remain optimistic. "I promise. Now spit it out."

"A young woman was seen headed to the old church. I'm pretty sure it was Emma," Henry said, cringing.

Bill was floored. He was torn between myriad thoughts. He looked at Henry, desperately trying to get his voice to work.

"I know I need to concentrate on the operation, but I can't help but be concerned for my wife."

"At the risk of jeopardizing our friendship, I'll say that we need to worry about her later. The operation is more important at this point. With that being said, I have a spotter watching her," Henry said, obviously pained over his words.

Bill shook his head. He knew that having to ignore the fact that his wife was potentially in serious danger would be agonizing.

"Brother, I told you that you didn't have to help with the operation, but now it's too late to back out—not saying that you would."

"I would never hang you out to dry, Henry. I'm in this for the long haul."

"I know you are. You're a good man, and I expected nothing different," Henry said as he nodded.

Kramer was angry to the point of being viewed as a madman. He had slung material out of Spangler's desk all over the floor. He was looking for clues—things that would be an indication of what he had to face because of the actions that Spangler had taken. Fuming and spewing curse words, Kramer decided to check under the desk. He patted panels and felt for trapdoors.

Bingo! He had found the hidden panel. Kramer didn't even bother sliding it open. He smashed the panel with his fist, skinned his knuckles, and then unleashed a string of curse words. Inside the panel, he found the Enigma machine and the two-way radio.

"What do we have here?" inquired Kramer as he shot a glance over at the soldier. The soldier was unsure whether to answer the general major, or if it was just a rhetorical question.

"I asked you a question!" Kramer shouted.

"I apologize, sir. It looks like a two-way radio."

"Well, let's start it up and see what we get."

The soldier switched on the radio, and there was dead silence. The commandos were under orders to maintain radio silence unless it was absolutely necessary.

Kramer said, "Go downstairs and get me forty soldiers. We're going on a manhunt!"

"Yes, sir!"

"And when you are done, get back here. You are my personal assistant for the night."

The soldier saluted and ran down the stairs.

Kramer stepped out of the office and climbed down the stairs. The soldiers started to arrive and formed straight lines. Kramer stepped in front of the group and growled. "I want each and every one of you to die for the Nazi cause. Nothing is more spectacular than seeing your dead bodies holding empty weapons—because you used all your ammunition on the enemy. You won't be called brave or valiant because your death will be what you owe the Nazi cause. You will exit off the end of the east dock. Kill anything that moves. Now get out of my sight!" Kramer had clipped the two-way radio to his side and was listening for any and all activity. He moved toward the end of the east dock with his binoculars so that he could monitor the progress of the Nazi soldiers.

Kramer turned to the soldier beside him. "I didn't catch your name."

"My name is—"

"Like I care. Stay beside me and keep quiet!"

The soldier nodded, afraid to answer otherwise.

As they approached the end of the dock, Kramer paused and raised his binoculars toward the old church. He smiled as he realized that he had run all the vermin out and hopefully had left them destitute—maybe even starved.

His eyes became fixed on a moving object above the ruins. He focused the binoculars and realized that it was a young woman.

"Soldier! Go to the church and bring me that young woman!"

"Yes, sir!"

The soldier ran off the end of the dock and began to make his way up the hill.

Henry's radio crackled to life.

"We've got some movement, sir!"

"Report?" Henry said.

"It looks like at least forty soldiers moving toward our position."

"Keep an eye out and report back to me."

Kramer raised an eyebrow. "Hmm. We've got company? I guess we'd better prepare." He picked up the other radio. "All soldiers in the facility, be prepared to be called into action."

Washington, DC

The War Room was a bustle of activity with all eyes on the electronic maps along the wall. Phones were ringing, and people were having conversations all over. Jim and Ed had found seats along the front desk in the room and had begun the long night of nerves and coffee.

"I'm so nervous I can barely stand it," Jim said.

"Steady there, old man. It's just another day in paradise," Ed said.

"A lot of people will lose their lives tonight—and I'm supposed to be steady? What does that even mean?"

Ed shook his head. He had to maintain the nerves for both of them, he supposed. There was no way that Jim was going to be calm, and there was nothing Ed could do about it.

"Nothing, apparently. You've done a good job, Jim. You can be proud of the lives that will be saved for the loss of a few. The *few* are those who volunteered for this operation. It's not like you stuck a gun to their heads."

"Nothing is ever going to make me feel better, but I'll get over it."

"I sure hope so, old friend. You'll make me worry otherwise."

"Less than five minutes. Hand me the coffee."

Saint-Nazaire

Emma had focused her attention on the activities on the docks and had not noticed that there was a Nazi soldier on the stairs leading to the perch. The soldier crept up slowly so as to not draw attention to himself. Emma was standing when arms surrounded her throat. The soldier stuck a knife blade against her neck. She gasped and instinctively rammed her elbow back into the soldier's midsection. There was a resounding "oof" as the soldier bent over.

The explosions at the docks began. The impacts from the detonations were so intense that they shook the old church. The stone had begun to crack, and there was dust everywhere. Emma held onto the stone rail of the perch as the soldier fell backward and dropped his knife. Emma released the rail and retrieved the knife from the floor. All sense of what was right or wrong had left her. All she was concerned with at that point was ridding herself of the threat. The Nazis had destroyed her hometown and had killed all her friends. People she had loved were gone. The town she had loved was gone. Tears streamed down her face as she stood over the soldier with the knife in her hand.

The explosions were becoming more intense as they worked their way from the west dock to the east side of the facility. The next explosion was so strong that it knocked Emma off her feet. She fell on the soldier, and in the process of the fall, she rammed the knife into his rib cage.

The soldier shrieked in agony. Blood had sprayed all over Emma. She removed the knife and began to stab him over and over—not even aware of what she was doing. The soldier stopped moving. He was dead. Emma stood up and collapsed backward into the wall. The explosions continued as they rocked the church. She didn't care if the church collapsed on her at that point.

The explosions had also knocked Kramer off his feet. He rose and retreated behind the barrels of napalm that Spangler had ordered to be placed on the east dock. By that time, a multitude of soldiers had fled the destruction— about fifty in all—and come back to the east dock.

Kramer stood up from his hiding place and surveyed the damage. There was a massive fire raging on the west dock as the ships that were in dry dock had been destroyed and had been a major cause of internal damage to the facility. A massive amount of metal submarine net had been scrunched over to the east dock and had seemingly formed a wall about twenty feet high along the railing.

"Go out—and get those who did this!" screamed Kramer. "If any of you survive this, I'll kill you myself!"

The soldiers scrambled off the end of the dock as machine guns began firing in the distance.

Kramer climbed up into the watchtower, which stood thirty feet above the dock.

The commandos waited until the explosions had subsided before advancing. The presence of the Nazi soldiers had thrown a wrinkle in the operation, especially since the commandos should have already been on the move. They had just begun to scramble out of the cave as the first wave of Nazi soldiers confronted them. The first five commandos were killed almost immediately—but not before they had taken out several Nazi soldiers.

Bill and Henry were getting ready to meet the onslaught of Nazi soldiers when there was a clamor outside. Three men burst through the hatch door and presented themselves. One of them was Alexandre. The other two were wearing Nazi uniforms.

Bill and Henry raised their weapons.

"Whoa, gentlemen!" Alexandre said. "These guys are friends!"

Henry said, "When's the last time you saw a friend wearing a Nazi uniform, brother?"

"I think that's what they call a cold day in hell," Bill said.

"Allow me to identify ourselves," said Dieter. Dieter introduced himself and his friend Klaus and explained who they were and why they were dressed as Nazi soldiers.

"We're here to help you, sir."

"We need all the help we can get," Henry said.

Emma sat next to the dead soldier and cried all the tears that she could stand to shed. He was a Nazi soldier, but she had never killed a man. Her anger turned to regret, and she wished Father Ambroise would magically appear to absolve her of her guilt. She had killed in self-defense, but why did she have to stab him so many times? Was it desperation in saving her own life? Emma sat in her self-pity and self-loathing, confused by her guilt and justification for taking a life.

The thirty-five remaining commandos began their trek back up to the bomber. They fired at targets behind them and those running up the hill There were thirty-five of them left, and their numbers were dwindling fast as the bullets were thick from the Nazi soldiers in pursuit.

Kramer stood in the watchtower, scanning the landscape and barking orders like his men were cannon fodder. "All soldiers move to the top of the next rise!"

The Nazi soldiers were a quarter of a mile from the top.

The Nazi soldiers were advancing, and they were less than two hundred yards away.

When the commandos reached the bomber, Henry yelled, "Blow the tree line!"

Bill leaned on the plunger, and the blast blew the trees clear of the plane. Bill immediately began firing the waist gun.

The Nazis were being shredded like wastepaper. Some of the bullets penetrated three and four bodies before they ended up in a tree. Bullets came through the window and rattled around the plane. Bill didn't even care if he was hit. He was determined to take out this foul bunch of wretched excuses for humans. The waist gun was empty.

Bill was ready to reload the waist gun when he realized all the targets were dead or dying.

Bill turned around to have a look at the damage in the plane. There were boxes spilled everywhere, and grenades were littering the floor. Bill was horrified to see Alexandre on his back, bleeding from his chest.

Bill knelt beside him. Henry knelt on the other side as they worked to stop the bleeding.

Alexandre smiled at Bill. "Take care of my daughter."

"That's quitter talk, Father!" Bill said.

"This may be all for me."

"The bullet hit you pretty high, so it probably missed your vital organs," Henry said.

Dieter and Klaus reentered the plane after the coast was clear.

Klaus said, "I've done medical work before!"

The radio began to crackle. "I'm waiting for you … Bill! You can come see me—or I'll go after your wife. You know where to find me. And just so you know, that was some fancy shooting on that gun."

Henry nodded and said, "You need to go."

Bill removed his M1911 pistol from the holster, checked the bullets, and put it back in the holster.

Alexandre took Bill by the arm and reached down to pick up a grenade. "You'll need this. Put it on your belt. This is what I saw in my dream."

Bill nodded his head as if he understood what Alexandre was talking about. In reality, he had no idea what he meant. He put the grenade on the back of his belt and bolted out the door as he headed to the docks.

"We need to remove the safeties from all the bombs and set the timers for the plastics," Henry said as he watched Bill running for all he was worth.

"Godspeed, my brother."

Henry truly hoped that Bill would rescue Emma.

Saint-Malo-de-Guersac

The windows rattled, and Josephine watched the ripples in her coffee cup. She was seated between Abraham and Jeanne and held their hands as they prepared for heavier shock waves. She had sent Sophie and Alise to the church with Father Ambroise.

The shock waves came in a rhythm, the windows rattled each time the waves hit, and the dishes danced on the shelves. After the shock waves stopped, Josephine let out a long sigh. All was safe, and very little damage had occurred.

Saint-Nazaire

Henry, Dieter, and Klaus were working feverishly to deactivate the safeties on the bombs. The pinwheels were designed so that the bombs would become active after they left the plane. After they were released, the wind would spin the wheels. This design kept the bombs from exploding as they were being loaded or being transported to the target.

Once they completed the activations, Henry set the timer for thirty minutes. That would give them time to get outside of the two-mile perimeter before the detonation. The fireball would extend out to about a two-mile radius, and God help anyone caught in the firestorm!

Emma was still seated on the floor of the perch with her arms wrapped around her knees. She was afraid to move. The fighting had been fierce, and she didn't dare put herself in danger by being a spectator. The tears had stopped, but they had brought no consolation. They were just tears of deep sadness mixed with tears of great fear.

Bill was close to the dock when he looked at the old church. He was torn between going to Emma and facing the demon. General Major Josef Kramer needed to be stopped, yet Emma was in danger. His love for Emma was incredibly deep, but his hatred for the demon was equally as deep.

"I'll be back to get you, my love," Bill said, hoping she had in some way heard his words.

As he turned back to the dock, he heard a voice.

"Halt! Lay down your weapon!"

It was a Nazi soldier. Bill immediately fell to the ground and grabbed his pistol. He fired several rounds, and the soldier fell. The soldier squeezed off a few rounds of his own and struck Bill in the right shoulder with two of them. Bill cried out in pain and rolled onto his back. Holding his shoulder with his left hand, he pulled himself to his knees. He tore off the tail of his shirt and wrapped the wounds.

Emma heard the shots, and it snapped her out of her trance. She scrambled to her feet and scanned the area with the binoculars. There he was! She saw Bill on his knees, bandaging his wounds. He'd been shot, and she was desperate to go help him. She scrambled down the stairs and ran out the front of the ruins without a worry about her own safety.

Bill finished his bandages and moved into what appeared to be a smoke screen shrouding the east dock. The ominous smoke engulfed the area as the air currents moved in and made a swirling circle. Bill stepped into the shroud and continued to walk forward until he was on the dock. The smoke wasn't too thick and had surprisingly not choked him.

Emma had run for all that she was worth at the same time the soldier transports were landing on the shore. Hundreds of Nazi soldiers were disembarking at the cove, and she dropped to her belly at the edge of the smoke shroud so she wouldn't be seen. She watched as the soldiers climbed the hill and passed the church. They were headed for the bomber.

Henry had taken turns with Dieter and Klaus in the arduous task of getting Alexandre to safety.

Alexandre let out a loud groan and collapsed to the ground. "You'll have to go without me! I can't make it!" Alexandre said with all the force he could muster.

"We're not leaving you here," Henry said. "We'll carry you if we have to."

Dieter and Klaus grabbed Alexandre's body and began to trot. Alexandre was in great pain from the bouncing, but he decided to take his pain like the man he truly was.

Henry said, "I know you're in pain, sir. Please bear with us. We'll get you to safety and get you the help you need."

"You need to leave me," Alexandre said.

"No, sir! We leave no man behind." Henry was partly right. He and his crew had left Bill and Emma, but it had been Bill's decision to stay and face the incredible fight.

Bill stood at the edge of the smoke screen as he surveyed his surroundings. The smoke was in a swirl around a relatively small area of the dock. The detonations that had destroyed the facility were feeding a large amount of black smoke to the east end of the dock, and the fire that was still raging on the west dock was causing a convection of air that had created the swirl.

Kramer stepped down from the watchtower and stood in front of Bill. He was about forty feet away. "We have what appears to be a theater here … Bill. We're alone inside this swirling mass of smoke. It is inaccessible from the sea because of the submarine net."

Bill chose not to respond. He still had his weapon drawn.

Kramer looked at Bill, then to the pistol, and then back to Bill. "You know, I'm not afraid of death … Bill. You have a free shot. Fire away." Kramer spread out his arms.

Kramer's palms faced upward, and his smile was all too familiar to Bill. He looked at Kramer to see that his feet were together. He appeared to be a picture he'd seen before of a figure being hung on a cross. The nightmare was recognizable, but this wasn't the right setting. At least not yet.

"Your window is closing … Bill! Shoot me already!"

Bill pulled the trigger, but all that was heard was a click. His pistol was empty. He fumbled around in his pants pockets, but he had been in a hurry to leave the bomber and had forgotten to bring clips.

Kramer laughed and continued his mirthful laugh for several seconds. "This is too precious! You forgot how to count. I counted the rounds you fired at that soldier as I watched you from the tower," said Kramer as he continued to chuckle. He pulled the Luger from his waistband and fired at Bill.

Bill grunted in pain as he fell to the dock. The bullet had struck him in the right leg, and he doubled over in pain.

"I would certainly hope that I have your attention, Bill." Kramer moved closer.

Bill noticed that Kramer hadn't paused before stating his name. To him, the change was very ominous. He wasn't sure what Kramer wanted, but it couldn't be good.

A shape appeared in the smoke screen. As it approached, it was apparent that it was the wounded soldier. He was doubled over in pain and covered in blood. "Should I kill this man?" the soldier asked.

"No. But answer me one question."

"Anything, sir."

"Why did you disobey my order?"

"What order, sir?"

"The order that you were to die in battle!" Kramer lifted the Luger and fired a round into the soldier's body.

The soldier collapsed on the dock.

Kramer walked over to the dead soldier and pumped six more rounds into his body. He put the Luger back in his waistband, walked over to Bill, and knelt down beside him. "I have one round left. See? I know how to count."

Bill remained silent. He had resigned to death once again. He didn't care whether Kramer killed him. He didn't care whether Kramer made him suffer before death. He felt deeply at the mercy of Kramer, and he felt as if he were a failure at defeating him. Bill reached down and retrieved the blade that was strapped to his leg. He didn't point it at Kramer; he just grasped it in his hand as if he may need it in his own defense.

Kramer laughed. "You Americans and your movies! You brought a knife to a gunfight? This just keeps getting better and better! Now, down to business, my son," said Kramer in a serious tone.

Had Kramer just called him ... son? thought Bill.

"Whether you want to believe this or not, you are like a son to me. You are brave. You faced me down when we were at the church. You came after me when I made the threat to kill your wife. You knew I would have killed her, but you chose not to save her and come after me instead. Why, Bill? Why?"

Bill remained silent, partly because he was in pain and partly because he just didn't deem Kramer deserving of an explanation.

Still Kramer persisted. "You've never talked to me, Bill. I don't understand your apprehension. You're obviously not afraid of me." Kramer waited on an answer, but Bill remained silent.

"I'll make you an offer, Bill. If you refuse the offer, I'll have no choice but to kill you—and I don't want you dead. I know that sounds strange coming from me since I have no regard for anyone's life, but you can take my word that I don't want you dead."

"Why would you bother to keep me alive?" Bill asked. "I knew you would have killed Emma. I knew you would have killed many others if you were given a chance. I had to do everything in my power to stop you."

"He speaks."

Bill once again went silent, waiting on the answer to his question.

"Since you've graced me with your question, I have the obligation to answer it. My reply directly ties to my upcoming offer."

Bill was totally confused by this point. Kramer was going to spare his life if he accepted some offer? What offer could this demon of a man have?

Kramer looked down at his hand and drew a breath. "I'd like to offer you a chance to join me. Hear me out!"

Bill closed his eyes as he could only imagine what Kramer had planned to say to sweeten the deal.

"We would be a great team together, Bill. I could teach you German. We could get you a whole new identity. We could be rich!"

Kramer had totally lost his mind to think that Bill would be swayed by anything that came out of his evil mouth.

"Does your brain even hear what your mouth is saying?" inquired Bill.

Kramer's face wrinkled with the thought that Bill wouldn't find his offer attractive. No one had ever refused anything that Kramer had suggested, probably since they were afraid of him. But Bill was certainly not afraid.

"I'll tell you something, Bill. When I was in boot camp a few years ago, we were given a puppy to raise and feed. At the end of the boot camp, many of the soldiers had become attached to the animal. We were required to shoot the dog on the last day of boot camp. I didn't have a problem killing the dog, and do you know why?"

Bill shook his head.

"It's because I really don't think I have a soul. I opened myself up to you, and you rejected me. Now … I don't have a problem killing you." Kramer rose up and turned around. He walked to the edge of the smoke shroud next to the watchtower.

The timer counted down, and the explosion was deafening. Even from two miles away, the concussion wave reached Emma. The intense wind uprooted trees, and the heat of the fire ring was fierce. The screams of terror from the Nazi soldiers turned to screams of agony as their bodies ignited. Their screams turned to silence as hundreds of soldiers died.

The detonation knocked Henry and the others off their feet. Henry's arm looked broken. "Ah, great! I guess if this is my only injury, I'll consider myself lucky!"

The trees had been toppled a short distance behind them, and they could hear the crackling sounds of burning timber.

Klaus said, "I guess we had just the right amount of time to get away from that blast."

"We need to get moving," Henry said as they collected Alexandre and hobbled toward the city.

The blast shook the house pretty badly. Josephine had her eyes closed. She was clutching the hands of her two friends, Abraham and Jeanne. The windows rattled violently, and a couple of panes broke. At least a half dozen of their dishes had been knocked off the hutch and shattered against the floor. They had weathered the blasts, and that's all that mattered.

Bill had to shake the cobwebs out of his head as his ears rang from the intensity of the blast. His vision was blurry, and he was thinking that he might have blacked out from the shock wave.

Almost as if he were dreaming, he saw the shape of a man appear from out of the smoke shroud. It was indeed a man. He was identical to the man in the picture Henry carried. Executive Officer Phillip L. Van Landingham Sr. was dressed in his navy blues as he had been in the picture. Van Landingham snapped to attention and saluted. Bill was still in his haze, so he wasn't sure whether it was his imagination that Van Landingham was there.

Van Landingham leaned toward Bill. "Lead the target."

After he spoke, he backed into the smoke and disappeared.

This scene was part of the nightmare. Was Bill imagining it? Had Van Landingham spoken to him? Bill had no weapons, save for the knife, so what was he supposed to lead?

Bill remembered the grenade on his belt. Stifling the urge to scream in pain, he reached back and retrieved it. He pulled the pin with his thumb and held tightly to the clip.

Kramer staggered to his feet. Blood trickled down his forehead.

Kramer said, "I see you and your people have covered all the bases."

"It's time to die, Bill. Do you have any last words?"

Bill drew in a breath. "Yes, I do."

"And they would be?"

Bill mustered every bit of strength and tossed the grenade. "Lead the target!"

The grenade had gone well wide of Kramer, who watched as it whizzed past him. Bill expected to hear a splash as the grenade landed in the water, but instead he heard a clank as the grenade hit the wall of the watchtower. The grenade bounced back onto the dock and was spinning like a top in front of Kramer. Kramer faced the grenade and spread his arms like he was going to fly. His palms were up, and his head was tilted back as if he were welcoming death. Kramer's last words were "Well played, Bill. Well played!"

The grenade exploded, and Kramer was flung into the submarine net. His head was wedged between the wires, and his arms remained outstretched.

Shrapnel had ejected from the grenade in all directions. One glowing-hot piece punctured a drum of napalm and began spewing a large flame directly at Kramer.

The flames cut through his body and radiated in all directions. They leaped out of his eye sockets and palms. His head swelled to the size of a pumpkin, and his flesh dripped onto the dock.

Bill grunted and staggered in a circle. The knife fell and clanged against the broken stone floor.

The drum emptied until Kramer's body was nothing but a skeleton. It fell to the dock in ashes. His spine disintegrated, and his skull shattered on the dock. The wires from the submarine net dripped into the ocean.

His nightmare hadn't been a nightmare at all. It had been a prediction. Why had he been selected to harbor such insight? He really didn't see himself as being pure of heart. He wasn't a saint. Why? This question was sure to haunt him for a long time.

Bill stood in awe of the victory over the demon. It shook him to his very soul. He had won the battle against all odds, and this miracle thrilled him to no end.

Bill smiled, and the smile became a chuckle. Soon, his whole body was shaking with laughter. Then the smile became a frown—and his laughter turned to tears.

Bill covered his face with his hands as the tears flowed. He had never cried for anyone or anything. He dropped to his knees and wept like a child. It wasn't a soul-cleansing cry. It was a sorrow that he would never be able to justify or understand.

Emma made it out of the smoke shroud and coughed and gagged as her watery eyes adjusted. She saw Bill and ran to him. She cradled his body and wept with him. The tears were finally a consolation. Emma was just grateful that her husband was safe—and that she was holding him.

For Bill, the nightmare had come full circle.

Washington, DC

The stats had been posted: 38 commando deaths and 432 Nazis deaths.

"Congratulations, Jim," Ed said.

"Congratulations for what?" Jim said.

"For a successful operation."

"Too many dead, Ed."

"There will be many more operations proving that death is the way of war."

Jim nodded as he packed his papers away. As he grabbed his briefcase to make the journey home, he said in a dejected voice, "Let's go start another operation."

We honor our troops with celebration and fanfare.
We salute them because they'll fight for us everywhere.
The world is a much safer place to be
Because of the brave who fight for you and me.
Our troops who fight battles are steadfast and sure;
Their bravery and determination will certainly endure.
Our brave troops fight fierce battles in spite
Of the horrors before them every day and night.
They protect our lands from shore to shore.
There will be more!

Printed in the United States
By Bookmasters